Animals in Peril

Animals in Peril

Stories
Ryan Kenealy

CURBSIDE SPLENDOR PUBLISHING

SYNOPSIS

Animals in Peril is a collection of stories that take place across the Midwest. The cast includes a coronary thrombotic shi tzu from Chicago, a junko that has just flown into a skyscraper, a decapitated skunk in Ohio, a runaway roan and many others. The stories also involve humans going through transitions, losing and finding themselves often in the reflection of the animals that surround them.

www.curbsidesplendor.com

CURBSIDE SPLENDOR PUBLISHING

Published by Curbside Splendor Publishing, Inc.,
Chicago, Illinois in 2014.

First Edition
Copyright © 2014 by Ryan Kenealy
Library of Congress Control Number: 2014944462

ISBN 978-1940430065

Cover and book design by Joel Craig
Cover photograph by Joseph Desler Costa
Watercolor paintings by Ryan Kenealy

Manufactured in the United States of America.

www.curbsidesplendor.com

CONTENTS

For Bertie, Jude and Callum

Resuscitation of the Shih Tzu

I WANTED TO PROJECT A STATE OF INDIFFERENCE TO Ann's return. I wanted to be smoking on the stoop when her taxi pulled up. I had to smoke five in a row, lighting one off the other in the half-hour wait for this effect.

Ann had every right to leave me then return on a sunny day in a taxi. We'd decided that our relationship should never impede us from further geographic exploration. We would not strangle one another. So I had no firm ground for self-pity. I would be indifferent to Ann's return, then try to fox something else out of her I could legally be angry about, and this would have worked had the shih tzu's heart not failed.

It was very hot the day Ann returned. The vapors of burning roof tar and gasoline squiggled the air in the two o'clock sun and the sky looked spattered with grease spots the way a stove looks after bacon's been cooked on it. In front of the stoop I watched through the vapors a lady in the passenger seat of a pickup truck fan her naked baby with a missalette from Our Lady of Guadalupe, while her husband sold pork rinds the size of car mufflers to my neighbors. The shih tzu sat splayed on the stoop next to me. I cut its hair short the day before so you could see vulgar patches of pink skin through his shorn salt and pepper fur.

Since Ann left, the shih tzu has growled at things like car alarms and the robotic sound of "The Entertainer" that the ice cream truck loops as it crawls through the neighborhood. He seemed too proud to need any consolation from me concerning his absent master. I stopped walking him weeks ago. I would let him out but sit on the stoop while he mawed confusedly through the small patch of grass in front, writing some forlorn note with his urine. He could wander off at any time and I tried to let him know he could—our relationship had no geographical boundaries.

A jolt ran through me when I saw the taxi turn down our street—taxis normally avoid the neighborhood so I knew it was Ann. The taxi slowed at different points and I could almost hear her in the backseat giving miserable directions. Somehow the shih tzu also knew what the taxi meant and let out a strangely pitched howl as if it were trying to hold back a much stronger howl and the noise let out was the sound of its repression. The taxi rolled to a stop in front of the stoop and with a mechanical click the trunk opened to reveal Ann's canvas bag. The shih tzu began to sprint without direction across the urine-soaked grass, indiscriminately revving a low growl. I was still smoking but the adrenaline from seeing her pay the taxi, seeing her bag pop up before me, numbed me to my crusted lungs. This was when I decided to nub the cigarette and walk to the trunk. The shih tzu growled at me while it ran clipped diagonals around my ankles as if it recognized my resignation, as if it were yelling: You pussy, don't you remember the plan?

I plucked her bag from the trunk, then shut it. Ann, still in the seat, turned at the sound of the trunk to see me and smiled. She grabbed her change, exited the taxi, then stutter-stepped quickly toward me in her cork-bottomed heels. I saw the peach fuzz on her arms glistening, as the swarm of vapors intensified with taxi exhaust. I felt her unpainted lips against mine and her curled brown hair run over my shoulder. I pressed my head far into her and felt trembles spill out of her like laughter; that's when I heard the gurgled noises of the shih tzu. Ann heard them too and through this impossible confluence of emotions that the small sausage body of the shih tzu could not bear, we saw it on the sidewalk—its legs convulsing in the air.

Ann was first to the shih tzu. She reacted by placing her hands on her face like Olive Oyl might. I leaned down to the still-convulsing shih tzu. Our neighbors watched from their card table as I placed my hands on its small hairy chest and without thinking began compression. My hands were flush to its ribcage, with fingers up; most people don't know to do this and end up breaking the victim's ribs. Ann was covering her mouth, trying to keep her shrieks at bay. The shih tzu was no longer breathing and I wondered what it'd be like to have a dead shih tzu in the apartment, to move it around from the couch to the kitchen, to lift its dead head above the water bowl, to ventriloquize growl noises while pulling its black lips above its teeth.

On the third compression, the shih tzu coughed out a breath, which meant I didn't need to unseal and blow into its lips where a bit of foam seeped at the corner. We needed to get it to a vet.

Taxis will not pick up a man cradling a lifeless shih tzu. I explained this to Ann with different words, which made her face cringe around the eyes and loosen around the jaw as if she were about to have castor oil spooned into her throat. Our neighbors continued to watch us while breaking apart their pork rinds and splashing them with cayenne powder and lime juice. They own an old pickup truck with tall braces on either side of the bed. At the end of a normal day they'll have ten feet of bent metal stacked in it. But they weren't collecting that day. They were playing dominoes and watching us. Ann walked to their table and appealed to them in frantic hack Spanish for a ride to the vet. She has always been good at doing things like this. They stared at her nervously until a short and wobbly man with a mustache got off his chair and waved us to the brown Dodge pickup that had a dusty pink stuffed animal tied to the grill. I picked up the shih tzu. It was making strange noises and I was afraid to bring it close to Ann. Our neighbor told us his name was Jesús then drove us down the street to North Avenue en route to the vet.

The truck's lame shocks and struts bucked across the grated North Avenue Bridge where prostitutes liked to swagger during the wolfing hours. The river looked uneven and overgrown with nasty life and decrepit fences. Ann talked to the shih tzu in my arms telling it we were almost there, that it would be OK. The shih tzu let out a curdled noise, which made Jesús clench the wheel tightly.

When we reached the vet we offered rushed thank yous to our mustached chauffeur who said, "I wait, I wait." I told him not to and he was quiet, thinking it over. "I wait. I wait."

Like every vet hospital, the floors were a shiny laminate. I walked across the reflection of blurred fluorescent lamps, then handed the wilting shih tzu over to a man wearing a white lab coat. He asked a few questions, then walked to another room. Ann and I stood in the hallway not knowing what to do next. We didn't look at each other; we were afraid to. The receptionist put her arm around Ann, then gently led us to seats in the front room that was occupied by a sleeping greyhound and its owner who was reading a magazine.

We sat close to one another. My arm ran the length of her thigh and clasped around her kneecap. She began to cry. Her face was red. I hugged her as tightly as I could, she hugged back with equal intensity. I wasn't worried about the shih tzu, I was worried for Ann, and what I didn't know then was that Ann worried about the same thing.

Three months ago, Ann and I answered an ad in the paper calling for manual labor. The ad promised eight dollars an hour, free lunches and a chance to work for the European Circus. The next morning we sat on a curb outside a chain-link fence on Navy Pier with about fifty other people all hoping to work for the circus. At 9:00 a.m. a short French-looking man with a cigarette hanging from his lips rolled open the fence, then walked away. We followed him to a trailer and filled out forms. Shortly after we were bona fide circus employees and Ann wearing her tank top, jean shorts, and work boots began to do what she does.

I used to hate people like Ann—people who try so hard to find connections, who concoct bogus ones if none exist, but I got tired of dragging that hatred around. I kind of need people like Ann around me.

The first Eurocarnie she met was a man named Jacques who wasn't European at all—he was from Montreal but insisted Montreal was the same thing as Europe because he, like real Europeans, put a filter in his marijuana cigarette. Ann was mesmerized by this piece of exotica, this filter approach. She told me out loud in front of Jacques in an excited voice about the filter. "Oh, that's cool," I said lamely. And this shared social deviance was the beginning of a bond, something for Ann to snicker about with them. Jacques's purpose for illuminating this detail was different. He wanted to score some weed.

Lunch was a bucket of apples, sodas, and Hostess cupcakes. The scab labor and the lower-echelon Eurocarnies ate around the trailer and tried to talk with one another. I had a shirt on that people liked so people kept saying "that's a cool shirt" with big-toothed grins. I thanked them for the observation, not knowing how to build any conversation out of it. Ann interjected with "that shirt was his grandfather's."

By 3:00 p.m. we had some of the smaller tents broken down and everyone seemed happy to see the fruit of their work. Jacques decided the time was right to ask Ann if she could procure weed for him and his Eurocarnie cohorts. I was tying down some canvas when she asked if my friend Andrew still sold weed.

We left the pier weary and sundrunk at 5:30 p.m. It felt wonderful to be a part of the rush hour, waiting on the platform for the El with Ann and all the slouched men in suits and women teetering on their pumps. The communal summer weariness made me feel accomplished and proud. On the El I stared out the window, which held a thin reflection of my face shuttling over the blurring brown back porches of apartments filling with television light. I would look at this then at Ann's bare legs. She saw me doing this so she smiled and placed her hand on my thigh. "Can you call Andy when we get home?" she asked.

The Eurocarnies wanted three ounces—apparently they knew not to use the metric system when ordering up weed in the States. I called Andy. I hadn't talked to him in a while, so it was a bit awkward. He lives in the suburbs with his chain-smoking mother and his girlfriend. Because of our conversation's impossibly small radius, whenever I go to visit I spend most of the time looking into an aquarium at his collection of African fish that swim through a plastic skull.

"Three O-Zs—that's a lotta weed, man."

"Whatever you got is fine and feel free to, um, you know, gouge the prices a bit," I explained to Andy, which didn't excite him as much as hearing his future customers work for the European Circus.

That night Ann made us sandwiches and we ate them while watching Wheel of Fortune with the sound turned down and listened to a Gene Ammons record.

There's this thing Ann does when she wants to have sex. It's not very subtle. She'll poke with her index finger at my penis then smile. If I wish to do the same I'll also poke myself, then she'll pick it up as if it were a telegraph, and start talking like a machine: "I feel ready to do the devil's work how 'bout you. Stop." Then I'll volley back: "Armpits may smell corrupt but my hankerin' for you is not. Stop." It's a stupid process but it's quick and it works.

I could see the sun setting through the bay window as we rolled around. Her teeth, nose, and elbow made a vicious parallel as we shifted. She had this smile when she saw me acting aggressively. I saw her, the sunset, and Pat Sajak spinning under the slow repetitive hum of Ammons' "Ca' Purange" and I could be no happier.

Andy honked at 9:27 p.m. It was drizzling outside when I pulled the curtains to reveal his van idling on our street. Ann was more anxious than I and did nothing to hide it. When she grabbed her keys her face was all business.

Sliding open the side door of a van produces a scraping sound perfect for an entrance. Ann climbed in and I sat up front next to Andy. He's five foot seven and looked like a Muppet in the plush captain's chair of the van. We shook hands in that cool way you can shake hands with a person you don't know, then took I-90 through the rain while Ann chirped about how wonderful it felt to be in an automobile on the highway. And it is nice to be on I-90 as it bends before the black steel skyline of Chicago, but it's not that nice, and it was obvious Ann was over-nurturing the conversation.

We turned into the Presidential Towers, which looked like four tall sticks of margarine. There was a guard at the gate reading a bodybuilding magazine. He let us in but his eyes emitted an air of suspicion, perhaps because of the van.

This somehow planted the robust seed of paranoia in Andrew. The guard looked like a bodybuilder himself and this is not how Chicago police and security agents are supposed to look. They're supposed to be fat "and if you can't outrun them you deserve whatever sentence you get" is how a friend of mine explains it. There were more guards in satin jackets with walkie-talkies around the front of the building and Andrew felt that we should leave.

"They're not looking to bust weed-peddlers. They just keep the bums out and administer the lost and found department. We're on the same team—servicing the guest. Trust me," I told Andrew.

"What if this is a setup? You don't know these people."

"Andy. You're being ridiculous," I countered.

It took five minutes of this kind of talk to coax Andy out of the van with his backpack chock-full of Mexican red-hair.

Jacques was happy to see us. "Come in, come in," he warmly instructed. Ann led the way. We sat around a television broadcasting *COPS*. The Euorcarnies love this show, they explained, to which I shot Ann a look meant to express how wonderfully small the world really is. We watched intently as long metal Cutlass Cieras and Ford Thunderbirds raced and dipped, shooting sparks over dark pavement until the cops finally smashed them into a barricade, then squeezed what looked like a polyp of a tank-topped human out of the window and onto the ground where it was quickly shackled.

Ann seemed to glow in this company, giggling, and provocatively opening her mouth over their bong. Andy smiled like a father who had just ushered his daughter into the sacrament of first communion, feeling a sense of ownership and pride over the dull joy he'd just imparted. I was ready for the evening to end. I've never felt comfortable doing things like this, especially with the TV on to buttress any lulls in the conversation, but I tried to play along because Ann was so intent on impressing these people. At this point I should have made clear to her how stupid she was acting but I didn't, and why she acted this way wasn't revealed until later in the week when she made an announcement over lunch.

"They want me to travel with them to Atlanta and Florida."

"Who?" I asked.

"The European Circus," she said with a smile. "They're taking care of everything. I won't have to pay for food or shelter and they'll be paying me—money that I can save." I said next to nothing in response. As I explained earlier, I had no right to object. I should have brought up rent money and bills and all the other issues that require postage, but I couldn't even do this. She seemed worried I might be hurt that they didn't ask me along as well. She would be gone for three months, she explained, and I was to act as the shih tzu's guardian.

I stared at the silhouette our twisted bodies made on the laminate floor of the vet. For five minutes we held one another until a separate agony seemed to overtake Ann and she broke free of my grasp.

"I deserve this. I deserve this," she said. I reached back for her and she fell into me for a few seconds.

"I'm not a good girlfriend," she said slurping up her tears after she'd broken free of me.

"Stop talking," I said softly, but it didn't work.

"I don't deserve your support."

"Of course you do," I said.

"You don't know. I don't deserve it. I don't . . ."

"Stop talking, Ann," I said.

"No. There's something we need to talk about."

"No. There isn't, Ann. Not right now," I urged her. It was clear to me she'd done something, perhaps fucked an acrobat, and that sucks but she had no right to tell me now. She needed resolve; she needed to stop thinking in this old pattern. The world does not work this way, she is not being punished, the shih tzu's heart is no divine message. The shih tzu's heart failed because it was hot, because I neglected the thing, not for what she's thinking right now. I wanted to tell her this but I didn't, not because it wasn't clear, it was the only thing that was clear. I thought about slapping her, but didn't want to risk waking the greyhound and having it attack me. I tried forcing a stronger hug on her but this made her body recede into itself. "Do you want to tell me more?" I asked not hiding my exasperation.

"Don't you think I should?"

"No," I said which made her eyes bulge. Then something like laughter hiccuped out of her.

"No?" she repeated, sobbing and laughing.

"No," I said back. "It doesn't matter right now."

"What matters right now?" She asked.

I guess I should've said the shih tzu, but I never really liked the shih tzu until its heart failed so that didn't seem fair. Before I could respond we turned to the sound of the vet's footsteps along the corridor. He was holding the shih tzu, which was panting and trying to wrestle free. The vet walked over to us, then silently handed it to Ann who flashed a quick smile before walking with it to the counter where she laid down a credit card as if she were buying a loaf of bread. I stood next to her as she pretended I wasn't there. I followed her out to the parking lot where Jesús was waiting in the brown pickup. He opened his mouth wide, unable to hold back the large wave of joy the live shih tzu brought him.

§

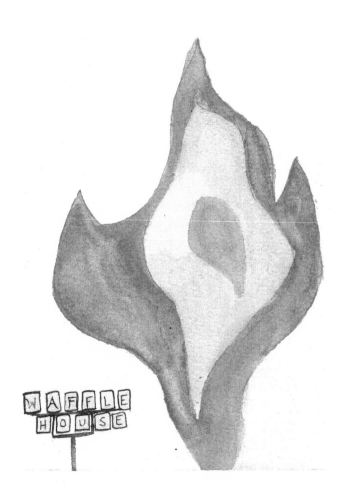

Uncle Dave

It all began with a Chevy Vega Uncle Dave hornswaggled from the insurance company, buying an obscure policy that protects families from fathers who go to jail, hours before my father was convicted. So it was a trade: my father for a red Chevy Vega. Uncle Dave drove us home from the courthouse, smiling toward the passenger then back seat as he turned into the driveway where the strange Vega sat. "That's a free car," my uncle Dave said, then coughed to my mother who had no reaction. We collectively approached the Vega, the same model that had rusted in the showroom, with trepidation; the world was swallowing our kin, maybe this was yet another sprung jaw. My brother was first to open the door. I got in next. Mom stood in front of the garage with her hands in her pockets staring vacantly. When she saw me she walked around to the driver side, opened the door and slid me over. Brothers Paul and Jerome climbed over the back, the place where I would later find a tin of hashish left by the previous owners. I remember the crumpled sound the vinyl seat made as my mother sat in its hold. I remember seeing the twinkle of her fingers over the wheel then that look; her eyes explaining that I was no longer a child.

Uncle Dave thanklessly helped mom with all matters fiduciary after dad's incarceration. Mom shelled herself in for a while, few people talked to her. The ones that did were always telling her how she must feel, then would embrace her as if patting deep into her ribcage the emotions they expected her to have. Uncle Dave never tried to plumb this; this was his charm. One night he came over with four bulging Ziploc bags pregnant with ridiculous jewelry. It was part of some scheme he was baking. My mother couldn't stop laughing. She was laughing at him, at his gumball jewelry, at this family she'd married into and at herself; she tried on the gaudiest things. My uncle was oblivious. He was smiling, thinking about the great deal he got. It'd been awhile since we'd heard Mom laugh like that. "Go on, pick out as many as you like … You know if you put these in a velvet box you can charge a lot of money." He went on to tell about an old friend who made home security systems that he tried to sell for 20 bucks apiece—"unsuccessfully … until he marked them up to over 100 bucks. He's got a boat now, drives a Lincoln."

My brothers don't remember Uncle Dave's efforts to make us happy when dad was taken away. The trips to Thistledown and Northfield Park watching the thoroughbreds and standards nicker in post parade at the Amish and winos along the rail. They remember how he distributed videotapes claiming Mormonism was a cult to family members in efforts to thwart the betrothal of my brother to his Latter Day bride. They remember how he would mutter inane, hypothetical asides as tacks to win arguments at family gatherings he was never really invited to "… and what if your boss doesn't fire the guy then the next day he comes in and starts knocking his penis against the wall of your wife's cubicle, then is he harmless?" But people go crazy for periods of time, like going under water. For Uncle Dave it took a while for him to surface. But before I explain this, I need to tell you about the arrangements he made to keep my soul pure.

Uncle Dave dated a former nun named Lucille. She was lanky and wore sandals. I heard my uncle telling his friend over the phone that he could write an entire novel with her pubic hair. He made preparations with my mother before asking me to join him, Lucille and another kid a few years older than me named Kevin, on a religious retreat down in Steubenville. He told me it'd be like a vacation.

Kevin sat next to me in the backseat smoking menthol cigarettes. His dad was some sort of business contact for my uncle. Kevin offered me a smoke, but I turned it down. Both my uncle and Lucille initially protested him smoking; he was sixteen, but he explained that it was part of the deal if they wanted him to go on some church trip. Kevin's parents were rich and he was spoiled, but I don't think he liked being rich or being spoiled and only acted that way as rebellion against the fact that he could act that way. About two weeks ago he snuck out of his house with a pair of nunchakis he'd fashioned from the handle of a Bissell sweeper and a bike lock. He walked through his subdivision bashing the fake gas lamps that stood over almost every rectangle of lawn. The cops didn't bring him to the station; they brought him back to his door where his robed father accepted him, a grand piano stood in the shadows like a giant insect about to pierce something.

Steubenville is four hours south of Cleveland. Dean Martin learned how to surreptitiously slip silver dollars into his loafer while dealing blackjack there. Steubenville, former hotbed of gambling, was now a magnet for the charismatic Christians that flood the Ohio River Valley. Like Al Green, the land inexplicably vacillates between moral righteousness and turpitude. The hills are what we noticed. Cleveland has none. My stomach enjoyed the exotic topography. On most of the hills stood three crosses made of plywood, sharing space with billboards of butter burgers crossed with bacon. Kevin and I got along well in the backseat. He read *Black Belt Illustrated* taking breaks to look at me, make a V with his index and middle finger then stick his tongue through the hollow. Then he'd laugh and point at me, "You know what that means. Ha ha, you know." I had no idea what it meant, but we got along well.

We stopped for gas in a town called Zanesville. Uncle Dave asked me to help check under the hood. His eyes swept across the oil, tranny and steering fluids. I held the rag while he plucked the sticks like a magician. He asked for a second opinion on each reading. They were all fine. "You don't think the oil has too much sludge in it?" he asked.

"I don't think so."

"Well, that's important. You can't be lazy about changing the oil. Do not learn that the hard way," he said, waving the stick like a maestro at me. Before pulling the prop rod from the hood, he looked at me and asked how I was getting along with Kevin. "Fine," I said. "Yeah, you're a good egg. I'd have a hard time with a rich little prick like that. You don't think he's a rich little prick do you?"

"No," I said. "Yeah, you're a good egg. Your dad always said that. Said that he didn't know where you came from, you thought so straight. He'd like to be taking you somewhere now you know. Bunch of fucking hypocrites," Uncle Dave said then looked away. He was referring to the people that put my dad away. "There's no good lesson to learn from it. There's nothing. You know that. You don't even seem to hate the people that put your father away, maybe you do," he said to me. My face sort of crumpled. "Look. Don't listen to me. I've never been good telling people anything about anything except shit like keeping your oil clean. Your dad's a good man and don't ever forget that. When I die I don't know if anyone will be around for it, you know. But he has a lot of support, a lot of people, even through this. He's made more good decisions than bad. And, you know what his best decision was. His best decision is standing in front of me right now."

"Listen," he said, leaning down to my height then pulling a circular tin from his pocket. "Look what I bought at this hillbilly gas station." Cigarette LOADS was printed in a white starburst. "You know what these are?" "Cigarette Loads," I said. "That's right." Now it's good you're getting along with Kevin, but there's something that needs to be done about his smoking."

The loads looked like tiny white headless nails. You slipped them into the tip of the cigarette and when the smoke was lit, the load would blow up. Uncle Dave told me I would have to get his cigarettes from him at some point and shove as many as I could into one. He said the effect was better if you could get three or four in.

* * *

Six big tops were set up in the middle of a meadow perched over a series of undulating hills. The adults stayed at the Howard Johnson down the street, Kevin and I would set up quarters under one of the big tops. We could hear a man preaching as we walked our sleeping bags and packs to the tent. He kept repeating "Don't be deceived, don't be deceived." The sleeping tent was filled with rows of cots. One cot held a kid about our age lying down listening to some sort of metal on a thin ghetto blaster. Most of the cots were taken, but two were free near the kid. We put our stuff down. Kevin lit up another nonloaded smoke, walked over to the kid and said hello. The kid nodded and raised his hand. Kevin noticed the speakers of his thin ghetto blaster were bent inward like a Caribbean drum. He asked the kid how they got that way. Without saying anything the kid took the thin stereo in both hands and smacked it against his head three times.

The air in Steubenville felt hot and thick, like it does around the fourth of July in Cleveland. Kevin asked the kid with the thin ghetto blaster to join us as we walked toward the big top that swelled like a fresh welt out of the dried mud. The kid's name was Justin. His mom sent him here while she went to visit her boyfriend in Cincinnati. The preacher kept with his mantra. Backlit in the big top's penumbra was an image of Pope John Paul holding a crucifix-topped silver staff. The preacher kept pointing at the image when shouting his refrain; he was condemning some rock 'n roll music no one listens to anymore. We walked to the lip of the tent. It was packed with people slowly waving programs below their faces. No seats were available. A few groups sat on the grass just outside the tent. We found our way to a patch of grass and had a seat. A smiling usher came over to hand us a program. The frozen image of John Paul on the Jumbotron made him look like a giant rat about to thwack the gesticulating preacher with his crucifix. It made me think about the cross and something my father once said to me after he'd won at cards: What a man is willing to wager is more important than the cards he has to play. It wasn't all of Jesus' great ideas that are glinting in the televised sun, it was the crucifix.

My favorite religious symbols involve animals. Everyone's seen the fish, but I like the pelican that's carved on the altar of the cathedral downtown. A pelican will slice into her belly with her beak to feed her young if there's no other food around, or so the myth goes.

"Excuse me. Excuse me," a girl's voice came from behind us. We all turned around to a girl who, while trying to scooch closer to Kevin, gave the most plumb beaver shot I'd ever seen.

"Can I buy a smoke off you?"

"No, but you can have a smoke," Kevin responded, explaining that they were menthol. Justin piped in something about menthol being made out of small shards of glass that will sit in your lungs for decades. The girl tucked the cigarette behind her ear in a way that made the three cigarette loads I'd jammed in plain to see. Kevin continued a line of small talk with the girl. She was sitting with one other guy and one other girl, as I stared in sphincter-tightening fear at the mouth of her cigarette. Would it go off right here? No. I would not let it get that far. They were also here from Cincinnati with a youth group. She mentioned that she was trying to talk Rob, the guy in their group, into driving to buy some smokes. She mentioned the food here was terrible and that she saw this Waffle House on the way up. Kevin turned to Rob and said he'd get him a pack of smokes if he drove. This was met with silence. "I'll get you three packs of smokes."

Rob was quiet for a little while then his eyes seemed to brighten. "OK," he said.

"It can get a little boring during the day, but it's a lot of fun at night when we speak in tongues," Carrie added.

"What?" Kevin came back.

"Yeah, everyone speaks in tongues at night," Justin responded.

It'd been decided we'd have to suffer through the rest of the preacher, but after that we'd go to the gas station for smokes with these Cincinnatians. The van made a throaty noise as if it too needed a pack of smokes from the gas station. Inside we felt a strange giddiness at our collective fast acquaintance. Rob was driving with both hands on the wheel. Kevin and I sat next to Justin in one row of the van and in front of us Carrie and Deanna kneeled in their row facing us. My foot twisted in the plastic pop container and wrapper roadtrip detritus that lined the floor.

"What's the speaking in tongues like?" Kevin asked.

"You'll see. It's weird. People pass out and stuff," Carrie responded.

"Sounds awesome. Has anyone ever said anything like 'Hail Satan' by accident?" said Kevin.

"Naw, it's just a lot of nonsense talk," Carrie said.

"Something you might be good at," rejoined Deanna.

The gas station had colored pennants strung lifeless in the summer doldrums, the multi-colored fangs of Steubenville. Rob looked at us in the rearview mirror and said he'd like a pack of Basic Lights. Across the street in block letters 80 feet in the air read: WAFFLE HOUSE.

"Oh, we gotta go there," Carrie said. "They have Chicken and Waffles."

It would cost us a plate of chicken and waffles, but Rob was easily cajoled.

There was a station wagon parked in the Waffle lot. In front of it a man sat on the curb with green tint wraparounds and a button that read "Ask Me About Jesus." He didn't flinch as we walked past him quietly listening to the clinking of hot engines at rest. Thankfully, no one took the bait pinned to the man's shirt. I thought about Uncle Dave; he might be a little worried about where we were.

We weren't sitting five minutes before Carrie asked us with the smile of a wizened monkey why we'd come to the retreat. I figured I held the most exotic card, having an incarcerated father and an uncle with a penchant for hirsute ex-nuns. I knew Kevin's story, or at least thought I knew it. Kevin reflexively shot back, asking them to answer first. He's going to be a good businessman in some phase of his life. The table was quiet before Deanna said it wasn't all about Jesus for her. "I come here because … the people are nice and don't judge you, don't hold anything over you. No matter what. See, the people where I live aren't like that; they can't make an original decision about you."

"I was forced to come here," Kevin said.

"I was forced to come the first time too," Deanna said as the waitress laid a plate of chicken and waffles before me. Everything in here was tan. The walls, the food, the chairs, the waitresses.

"I don't know anyone who would choose to come to one of these the first time, but I do know that the people that end up here are good, nonjudgmental people."

Kevin seemed as thankful as I to have a plate of food before him. We ate our chicken and waffles as one of the waitresses wearing a studded belt and spiky hair waved a silent vacuum over some carpet in the back of the restaurant. It was a tasty journey through solid and liquid tan. About midway through the meal Kevin kicked me under the table. I looked at him and he pointed his head toward Deanna then stuck his tongue through a V he made with his index and middle fingers then smiled at me. Deanna also saw him do this and stared at him. He looked at her then down at his chicken and waffles, then started giggling. Deanna shook her head. "So Kevin, why were you forced to come here?" she asked, then smiled and tilted her head at him. Kevin continued chewing his food, raising his index finger then wiping his mouth with his napkin.

"I'm here 'cause I'm a fuckup," he said.

"Yep. That's why I'm here," Justin said.

"Me too," said Rob.

The sun was less violent when we finished eating. On the ride back we listened to music with the windows down.

When we got back, I could see Uncle Dave and Lucille in folding chairs outside the big top. They must have figured we were somewhere within the throng. On stage a bunch of kids were acting out that old parable about investment banking. The dad gives his sons a bunch of money, and the one who buries it in the ground rather than invest is punished. It's one of the only parables that doesn't ennoble suffering or meekness.

Kevin and I split apart from the others. We walked over to check in with Uncle Dave. There weren't any open seats around him so I walked a couple rows ahead and waved at him. He waved back. Lucille glanced over. For some reason I expected them to get up and find out where we'd been. But they brought us here; their shepherding was complete.

* * *

After the parable there were "witnesses." People told sad personal stories. It must have taken a lot of courage to do this sort of thing. To be honest, I didn't want to talk about how I felt about my dad going to jail. I think my uncle secretly wanted this to happen. People had expectations for my disgorging of the psychic perils that travel with having a jailbird father. What I wanted to happen was the same thing I bet my dad wanted, and that was to be removed from the incident. I didn't want to talk to people or hear any similar stories. I wouldn't lie about my father or what happened, but that didn't mean I needed to tell everyone. It just made people nervous when I told them, made them not know how they should relate to me, and I hated watching people try to calibrate themselves so they won't offend my special circumstances. I never feel better after talking about my problems, at least not when people tell me I'll feel much better. The sun was setting behind a limestone bluff, the program listed two more events for the evening.

8:00 Tongues of Fire
9:30 Evening Prayer led by Fr. Briman

We were broken into groups for Tongues of Fire. There were about 50 others in my section. Carrie, the one who mooched the smoke from Kevin, was one of them. She sat next to me and put a hand on my knee, perhaps sensing the mix of terror and curiosity in my eyes. I remember her welcoming flash of white teeth and eye. The priest began to ask the Lord to be with us. To lead us and protect us. To make us understand and be a part of Him. It was hot and humid even after the sun left. Things felt pushed together and intermingling, but not in an oppressive way, like time was bubbling. A large woman stood up from her folding chair and the priest walked over to her holding an open missal that looked like a soaring bird from a bad watercolor painting. He placed his other hand over her head. She spread both arms as if checking for rain, then mumbled a few things that didn't make sense. I listened closely. Her eyes were closed as she rattled off sounds that rose and fell. A few long seconds later she crumpled to the ground. People had cleared away chairs in anticipation of this. Someone caught her on the way down but only managed to break the fall. People grouped around her doing the sign of the cross and praying. The priest moved away and kept intoning the Lord to vouchsafe the spirit and lead. Shortly after an old man stood up and the sequence repeated, only he didn't fall. He just sat back down with his arms cupped upwards. I looked over at Carrie who smiled at me. She put my hand on her leg and rubbed it up her thigh. Her thin leg was soft yet it seemed to reveal the sharp architecture of her entire body. It would take a while to sort this moment out, but the last thing anyone in the group wanted to do was think. If you wanted to be a part, you had to allow yourself to be swallowed and have faith that the Lord would vouchsafe. More people stood, some collapsed, some sat back down. I thought about trying it, just to see what would happen. I wanted it to work on me, to stand then fall, and I felt like I could blackout, and that maybe it'd be good for me. Something I could do that people wanted me to do. It was hot enough. Carrie leaned into me and asked if I wanted to leave and meet up with Deanna and Kevin who arranged to hang out in one of the meadows. Deanna had a Frisbee that lit up, she explained. I agreed and we left, walking outside of the tent into the darkness. People were clustered as if around bonfires. Some were praying, some were chanting, some were holding candles with paper saucers, others were holding hands.

I wanted more than anything to run my hand over Deanna's leg. In the distance I saw what looked like a red flame flitting back and forth in the sky. It was the illuminated Frisbee.

"Did you speak in tongues, dude?" Kevin yelled at me. Rob was sitting in the grass with Deanna. Justin was running after the Frisbee.

"I didn't," I responded, then opened my hands for the Frisbee. It looked like it was one of the first times Justin had run in a field, nearly tripping with every darting move. We tossed the disc around for about a half hour without talking much. Carrie sat with Deanna and Rob and watched us. Kevin could throw overhand and under and enjoyed watching Justin and I run for the red blur. I thought someone would come by, put an end to this, scorn us for our lack of piety, but we were left alone. Once you said your prayers and attended the functions, you were free. I worked up a nice sweat. It's amazing how good running in a field makes you feel.

We talked about different things in the circle. I learned that Carrie's father was a local weatherman in Cincinnati, something she didn't seem all that proud or ashamed of. I thought it must be weird to see your dad on the news every night, acting like a completely different person. Maybe it's a good thing to see your dad have more dimensions. Kevin kept asking about the bluff, asking if anyone had ever climbed it. It was something he clearly wanted to do and for the next half hour he tried to convince us of the worthiness of the mission. Carrie sat next to me, our hands in the grass. At one point she walked her fingers across mine.

I was lost in a moment with Carrie when I realized everyone was standing, heading to the bluff. Kevin was the leader with Deanna his lieutenant. He claimed to have seen a path that led up the hill to the bluff. The trail was full of magnolia trees and rhododendron, rubbery and ancient. The Frisbee lit the way. After a few bats flew by, Carrie grabbed my hand. I told her it was clear as day for them, they wouldn't fly into us or tangle in our hair. I pointed out to her what looked like large whitish wings that belonged to a barn owl. Once he found a suitable limb he started screeching for a mate. How did Kevin talk everyone into this? We reached a perch where you could see the big top in the distance. We were up about 50 feet. We sat down near the clearing. If we wanted to go any further we'd have to climb a rock face or forge a new path through brush laden with poison oak.

"I think we should go back and look at that owl. I've never

seen one up close," Carrie whispered into my ear.

Beaconless, we walked back toward where we saw the owl. He was still screeching. It was dark, but I could see his silhouette. "There he is." Carrie brushed her hand over mine then looked at me with tightened lips. We stood there for a little while. I put my hand on the side of her hip and cupped it around her waist. She had small hips. I wanted to lift her off the ground and push her into me. She moved in for a kiss. It was long and quiet and I could smell her makeup mixing with the oils on my face. Our hands explored each other for a long time. I remembered a friend explaining that when you're rounding third base, you want to use your index and ring finger to skirt the edges, then dive in with the middle. I employed this technique and my advances were met with heavy breathing. I got close to her face and asked if she thought what we were doing was wrong. I'm not sure why I said this. Her eyes darted around, her body stiffened, and I realized I just said something stupid. I needed to lead the quest, to vouchsafe her with the spirit. Without speaking she got up from where we were sitting and began to walk away. I waited for a little while then followed her. I called her name but she didn't respond. I'd never felt so incredibly stupid and confused. She got to the clearing and saw no one, so she began to scale the rock face. Scree was falling around her. "Carrie," I shouted, but she was half way up and had no intention of returning to my level. The rock face was almost vertical. I was never good at climbing. But I decided to scale it and at least catch up with Carrie to smooth things over. What would she tell the rest of them? I was half way up when my foot slipped. My body shook nervously and was feeding on that energy. I realized I could easily fall and roll off the clearing, that this was really stupid. I could die all alone after being with these people I didn't know in a place I didn't know. I started sweating and could smell Carrie on my hand, which shook me out of the nervous loop and gave me a strange feeling of confidence. I needed to calm down, to shake everything off. I was more than halfway up. My breathing got a little slower. Without thinking I began my ascent, a series of repeated motions. I threw my leg over the ledge and clambered up. This is when I became aware of myself again. I could see the big top way in the distance like a moon. For about five minutes I just stood looking at the sky and the tents, feeling inexplicably exultant, as if the reason for my trip had finally made itself known. Then I heard Carrie ask what I was doing.

I turned around and saw her sitting with her arms wrapped around her legs. "What are *you* doing?" I countered. She didn't answer. Instead she put a cigarette in her mouth and started flicking a lighter, casting a yellow light over the cigarette that held the three loads.

"Wait! Don't light that!"

She had the lighter lit and was staring at me, then slowly pulled it toward the cigarette. She wanted me to know she was past the point of listening to me.

§

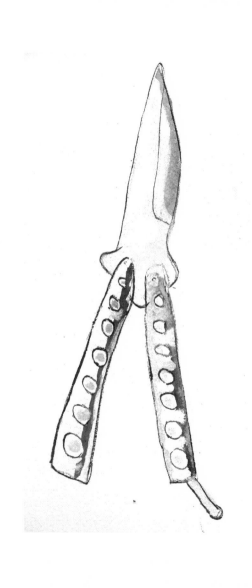

Flea

THERE WAS A SENSE OF SATISFACTION FROM MY KNUCKLES striking the baby fat around his cheekbone. A hit that direct actually hurts less, but I knew it would bring him down, the momentum alone would. The crowd reacted. They felt something different from satisfaction. The opposite actually, they wanted blood. And that's when I walked away. Down the forest path that ended in birch trees pointed like tusks at our subdivision. I ran to my empty, silent house, dropped my backpack and went straight to the garage for my bike. I pedaled furiously down the street, cutting through the dirt veins of the park. Pussy willows sprouted up on either side, funneling me into the Dairy Queen parking lot then onto the main road. I didn't have to think at all about what anything might have meant as long as I was pedaling. Smoke poured from the steakhouse where anniversaries and homecomings were given the nod with lattice-branded steak, sent up with a billow of beef smoke that curtained my neighborhood from the next, the one I wasn't allowed into. The one whose far border was near the airport, the salvage yards, the massage parlors with oriental names. The road atomized into gravel. I wasn't thinking as long as I was pedaling. Up ahead I could see a reflection of the sun, usually soft at this hour, somehow redirected sharply onto what looked like a heat shield haloed with a Pontiac crest. I pedaled toward the light, no longer sweating at all, just moving closer to the light.

* * *

I don't regret punching him. He deserved it. But I hated feeling the crowd that gathered. They had nothing to do with it. I wasn't trying to make a public statement about not messing with me. But there was more. The fact that I could feel the impulse of the crowd scared me. I could let these people press me into something I didn't want to be, something for their pleasure. That disgusted me.

* * *

I kept pedaling toward the light as I felt my body falling away. My eyes closed as my bike folded underneath me and I rolled onto some grass. For a few a seconds there was only darkness with tiny blue and gold lightning strikes flaring under my eyelids. About five yards ahead, hubcaps reflecting the sun hung in netting that jutted out from the southeast corner of a pink and gold building. The bejeweled web looked like something that would be sent into space. A man with Jheri curl ringlets hanging down from a beret waved smelling salts under my nose as I stared at the glinting hubcaps that drew me here.

He asked me my name, what year it was. Others came out of the flea market to see if I was OK. One of them was Qasi. Pronounced Casey.

Qasi moved to Cleveland a couple years ago. German priests helped him get out of Iraq, where he was held prisoner for being friendly with a young band of rebels who wanted to overthrow Hussein. He was not friends with any band of rebels and still wonders at least once a day why his name was given. He knew who had given his name. He'd done nothing to him. He was tortured by guards thirsty for more names, and he figured so was the guy who'd given his name. It was just random, brute force carried out. His family was Assyrian, and they were able to get help from priests. While he was imprisoned, his mother died from a mix-up at the pharmacy. The priests took pity and moved his case to the front. They were able to extricate him from the prison and shuttled him to Amsterdam where he was granted asylum. After this any contact would put his father in serious danger. His father was a popular merchant. He was good at importing items that would lead to officials eventually banning them. Undeterred, he would move on to something new. He sold to regular people, but unlike the other vendors he didn't stock ersatz handbags or watches meant for conspicuous consumers try- ing to broadcast a wealth they didn't possess. His father was a salesman willing to risk his ideas. And he was forced to tell everyone his son had abandoned him, just as he'd abandoned his country. It was the only way to keep everyone safe.

Complications in Europe pushed Qasi into America, where he had some relatives who lived in Cleveland. The relatives took him in and helped him get a stall at the flea market—the flea market where I am currently lying in the grass.

Aloysius is the name of the man waving the smelling salts under my nose. I sat up and tried to stand but he put his thick chalky hand on my chest and told me to stay on the ground 'til I got my "winds." I wasn't in any pain but felt exhausted, hollowed out, more than I'd ever felt before. You bring up every part of yourself in a fistfight. They asked if I needed to go to the hospital and I knew not to seem too scared by the idea, so I calmly explained that I hadn't broken anything and wasn't bleeding. They thought about it for a little then decided I should call my parents. I used Qasi's cellphone to call my dad, but I knew he wouldn't pick up. He was at the gym and so was my mom. They were trying to grow old gracefully, they explained to me in the car once. While squatting over me they discussed what they could do next as the hubcaps behind them plated the catfish-colored late afternoon sun.

They brought me inside to Qasi's booth. He sold things like itch powder, whoopie cushions and switchblade combs that he displayed on a black cloth. He tried to offer me a piece of trick gum, and I thought about taking it just to make him happy, but waved my hand and smiled at him. He let out a belly laugh, "a smart boy, such a smart boy." In the next booth over, an old man slept in his chair as motionless as the belt buckles and incense sticks that surrounded him. I could see the row of brown sticks labeled Lavender, Patchouli, then one with a pink handle that read Pussy.

"See this," Qasi said, palming a silver disc with a button in the middle then pulling out a wire from the bottom of it. Once he had the line out he pulled a dollar from his wallet. "I'm going to share with you my greatest trade secret," Qasi said as he grabbed the nub at the end of the wire and stuck the dollar to it, then winked at me. He planted the dollar on the ground and retreated back to his perch. He glanced sideways at me, placing his index finger across the bottom of his nose, like a mustache, which made us laugh. He laughed without knowing I was laughing at the fact he didn't know how to make the shh sign. We waited for a while, like eagles on a branch scanning for field mice, but most of the people probably already knew the trick. Finally, a kid a little older than me walked by and bent down to pick it up. Qasi was quick on the button. I could see the boy making mental calculations as Qasi's eyes lit up, and he beamed a smile at his quarry as the dollar whirred back into his palm.

There was a large curtain behind Qasi that draped off a bookcase. The velour curtain whispered its summons. On the shelves stood a lurid rainbow of pink, purple, peach and onyx colored dildos in front of their boxes, pointed towards the heavens. It was very similar to the way a weird kid I knew displayed his *Star Wars* figurines. I grabbed a purple one and twisted the back but nothing happened. I smacked it, but still nothing. I held it against my cheek. It was cold and rubbery, reminding me of the armrest on the backseat of my parents' car that I'd rest my head on during long drives spent listening to the rhythm of the wheel well. On another shelf butterfly knives sat with their handles spread as if curtseying. On the floor I saw the logo for Black Cat bottle rockets surrounded by cardboard tanks and birds with wicks sprouting out of their throats. I heard the cell phone inside Qasi's pocket ring so I moved from outside the curtain. Qasi turned to answer just as I emerged.

It was my father. I could hear his muted voice leaking into the air of the market. He sounded a little panicky, then confused then deeply thankful to Qasi. He said he would be there right away. Qasi relayed the news with a slight curl of smile and asked if I was happy to hear the news. I shrugged. He told me I had very good parents and asked me if I knew that to be true. I nodded and abruptly asked him if I could work for him. He laughed. I could help attract customers, do inventory, clean. He laughed more.

"Why would you want to work here?"

"I like it here. I could learn things here."

"You can learn things at school."

"Not really."

"Yes really."

My parents arrived with shiny post-workout faces. Near the entrance a man was cooking a piece of bologna on a George Foreman grill that was missing the top flap. My father seemed scared, surrounded by everything he opposed. He smiled through the wafts of hot slanted bologna when we locked eyes. Qasi was very excited to see them; he hunched over in fealty. He told them that I was very smart for my age and that he enjoyed looking after me. Maybe there was something about being in charge of me, of having to supervise me, or maybe he just had something in his eye, but he seemed emotional.

I didn't really know what to expect from my parents. They were excited to see me, but I didn't know how that would pour into the way they litigated the day's events. They didn't like Tom (the kid I'd fought). Thought his divorced parents were white trash and Tom was spoiled; the type of kid who would use split parentage to his advantage. And he did. And he was. Just as I wouldn't allow disdain I might feel toward my parents keep me from accepting their offer to get pizza. It was for them a celebration of my cut ties with Tom, but the ties weren't cut. In fact, twisting around in my head as we got off the parkway and entered the endless parking lot was how I was going to tell Tom about the flea market and Qasi and the bottle rockets and the butterfly knives. These are things we could easily sell to our classmates. It was an opening for us. I think part of the reason I wanted to be friends again with Tom was because it was the opposite of what everyone else wanted. So it would be all mine.

I ate an entire pizza and my parents seemed delighted. They looked at me like I was their prize colt who had just scarfed up all his oats after a demanding race. I played some Galaga on the tabletop arcade, staring at the thin reflection of my face covering the aliens I shot into circles of smoke.

* * *

I went to Tom's locker before class the next day. He had a nice bruise from the shot I'd given him. I asked him if it hurt. Not really, he said. Then I told him about the bike ride to the flea market. He didn't know why I was telling him this, but seemed to get a kick out of hearing about the smelling salts and the guy with the Jheri curl ringlets. Then I told him about what I'd seen behind the velour curtain. And his eyes lit up. He wanted to know if I was able to grab any. The flashes of excitement he leveled were tempered with another sheepish impulse to withdraw. That it didn't make sense for us to be friends right now. That it was too confusing. I wanted to quickly deploy my plan like a rampart over that. But it wasn't working, and he hung his head, not sure what to do with all the mixed up feelings he had. I curled my hand under his chin and had him look me in the eye. "Let's forget about what happened and be friends again."

* * *

Aloysius would stop by Qasi's booth and chat. Outside the Assyrian community, Qasi had few friends, and he was tired of the Assyrian community. He didn't feel any nostalgia for his homeland. That might happen later, but not now. Now he simply thought the place where he grew up was fucked up. He liked American food, music and women. He and Aloysius (never Al) became friends. Aloysius knew people at the flea market who could hook him up with bootlegs of movies and music. He knew people that went to clubs where electronic music throbbed next to the sluggish Cuyahoga River late into the night. He ate frog legs with Qasi at the all-night fishery. Some people say that there are magnets in the earth that let you know when you're in the right place. If that's true then those magnets aligned Qasi with Cleveland.

One rainy, gray spring day that felt sluggishly warm after a long winter, Qasi decided to close his booth early. The clouds hadn't roused from their winter bed over the eastern edge of the Great Lakes. Qasi was a little pissed because some frog-throated rednecks in the cafeteria kept talking about ragheads while they ate their brown food. It usually didn't bother him all that much. It was a choice, he told himself: whether or not you let these idiots bring you down. You can't educate them. But that buffer against the brown-food eating rednecks wasn't working, so he decided to leave and drove through the milky day to the fishery. The huge windows that looked out over Lake Erie were fogged over. Inside the fishery, the diffuse light created a warm white blur. He ordered the frog legs and took a spot in the corner where a bunch of people were watching Spider-Man. He sat and laughed at the stupid jokes with them. Maybe it was the quality of the light or the safe harbor. Maybe it was the swampy taste of the frog legs, a taste he never felt in the arid lands of the town he grew up in. But he felt at ease, and realized that anonymous contact with random people was something he needed.

* * *

People always want something from you, and you have to choose what you're willing to give (or trade). I wasn't willing to beat the crap out of Tom for the crowd. But I was willing to give them butterfly knives and fireworks, and maybe Tom would want to help. Initially Tom was unsure. He knew the risks of getting caught were much greater for me. His parents never grounded him and only yelled at him if he didn't do things like fold the laundry properly. It was different for me. He felt the scorn my parents had for him at sleepovers. He knew they didn't want him around their son and that hurt him, but not enough to not want to be around. Maybe he felt he could eventually win their acceptance or that he had to try. I can only guess.

My plan was for us to bike to the flea market on Saturday. I would introduce Tom to Qasi. We could then convince him to hire us for very little money; maybe we could even work for free as a favor for how he looked after me. We could inventory, clean, sell, whatever. Then we could work out a deal. We could work for merchandise or he could just sell some of the stuff to us. We would gather up a list of what our classmates wanted and charge double. Everyone would be happy. We also knew it was in our interest to establish what our customers would have to tell their parents if they were caught with the contraband. If they wanted us to buy for them, they either had to accept a story we provided or provide their own alibi upfront. We could even provide consultation in strengthening their stories. We would be very valuable and very popular and no one would fuck with us.

The bike ride seemed longer the second time, watching our orderly subdivision dissolve into angry furls of chain link fence, gravel and tan brick buildings. We parked near Aloysius's hubcap hut. I waved over to him and smiled. He narrowed his eyes at me and raised his hand in an unsure greeting. Not a great start. I decided not to walk over to him. We didn't really need to talk to him anyway. The market was packed, full of fleshy people filtering through the aisles. Commerce wattling onward. I couldn't make out Qasi. His booth teemed with kids and some weird-looking adults.

We waited 'til the crowd thinned out. Qasi was very surprised to see me. I introduced Tom as my associate then explained that since we were all very busy men that I would cut to the chase. I reiterated my solicitation for employment. Qasi laughed. I explained how far we'd ridden that morning. Qasi came around from the other side of the booth and put his arm around me.

"This is not a good job for you. No job is good for you, but schoolwork. You don't want to work here. Trust me."

I was persistent but fading. Qasi asked if we'd had lunch. He walked us out to the hot dog stand that faced a table covered with stacks of tube socks crowned with the jaundiced colors of Cleveland sports teams. We ate at a picnic table and watched shoppers cast their blobby shadows over the assortment of chicken cages, cast-iron pans, old tools and fishing tackle. Qasi wondered again what it was we wanted at the flea market. "It's an exciting place," I mustered. Tom just nodded while slowly undressing the foil from his dog.

"It is an exciting place," Qasi said. "But these aren't your people."

It was quiet for a while then Tom asked where the bathroom was. After he left, Qasi smiled at me conspiratorially.

"Do you want to be a businessman? A salesman? Is that why you like this place?"

"Yes."

"Good. Is it because you want to make money?

"Yes, I want to make money."

"But is that the only reason?"

"I don't know."

"I don't think it is. I think you are curious about people and you want to try to, what is the word, predict what they want in their lives. You want to help them, but not really. You want to feel like you know how to help them, that you have the power to help them."

"I don't know."

"Yes, that's it. You're curious and you want part of the action and you want money, but more than that you want to know that you can make money when you want to. Does that make sense?"

"Um."

"It will. Soon it will. You know the problem with businessmen today?"

"No."

"Money."

"Money?"

"Money. It makes them idiots. It makes them forget that it's not about money, it's about being a man, about being smart. It's about making decisions. It's about knowing what's important to people. And then it's about talking to them. Making them understand you, understand what's good for them. You can do that here, but why not stay in school and learn how to do it in bigger places with people who have money, people who don't want cheap crap. That's what they want here. And I don't mind. I was born to sell things. I will always sell things. If they throw me in jail, I will sell things in jail. Do you understand?"

"No."

"It's not something I can shut off. It's who I am, and maybe it's who you are. But why start here when you can start somewhere better? Somewhere without all the cheap crap. Do you know what I'm saying?"

Tom returned from the bathroom, ending our conversation. Shortly after we all stood up to leave. My plan was dying in my confusion. We said goodbye to Qasi, who smiled immensely at us. Tom didn't seem all that disappointed. Maybe it wasn't meant to be.

* * *

On the ride home, Tom turned into a church parking lot and pedaled over to a corner near a crabapple tree. He walked behind it, turned his back to me and unfastened his pants. He asked me in a loud voice if I wanted to see something. I told him I didn't, but he turned around anyways. His pants were slightly undone and in his hands were about 8 butterfly knives he must have stolen from Qasi's booth.

"Fuck," I barked, and he laughed. I thought back to that moment when I had him on the ground and could have beaten the living shit out of him.

Tom pinched his face as if exasperated by my petty morality. Tom has always found ways to get what he wants, and I usually love this. Defiance against stupid bullshit is funny and good, but this was not that.

"You're mad because I stole from the raghead, aren't you?" Tom said with a smile.

"I should have kicked your ass."

"But you didn't. Why? Because you're a pussy. How 'bout that? ... C'mon dude, I'm kidding. Unless you wanna fight me now," he said while flipping around a sparkling knife in his hand.

I want it to be clear that I was angry, but what happened next wasn't about my anger, it was an exploration of a karate move I'd seen. It was the possibility opening up for me. I knew Tom was an asshole, but I wasn't mad about that. Honestly, I thought the whole thing with Tom being an asshole was charming and funny.

Tom was standing *en garde*, smiling as I walked up and kicked him in the hand that held the knife, which shot out of his hand and flew into his cheek. It stuck in and he probably should have left it there, but instead he yanked it out and the blood flowed quickly. I had never tried kicking a knife out of anyone's hands or anything like it, so I was pretty stunned how it all worked. He tried holding his face to make the blood stop, but didn't seem to know how, so I grabbed his cheek and pulled the two skin flaps together. I'd never been this close to his face before. I remember it smelled disgusting.

* * *

At the flea market, Qasi noticed his knives were missing right away and somehow knew it was us. He knew the neighborhood I lived in. He knew that if someone's parents found their child with a butterfly knife that it would somehow come back to him, and that would be it. He got in his car and sped off in our direction.

In my suburb there are a few hunters and a few hunting accidents every year. A kid in our class got buckshot in his cheek and reveled in the attention and the added manliness it brought. Maybe this is how it would play out for Tom, but we couldn't get the blood to stop flowing from his cheek, and neither of us wanted to get in trouble so we stood around and watched the color leave his face and drip over the crabapples. We probably would have just stood there till he bled out if Qasi hadn't spotted us. He got out of his car and applied pressure to Tom's cheek. It bled less, but still bled. He handed me his cellphone and told me to call 911.

The paramedics stopped the bleeding quickly, then put him in the ambulance where he was allowed to play with the siren. Tom told one of the paramedics about the butterfly knife, and after being asked pointed to Qasi and said he got it from his stand at the flea market. Both Qasi and I stared in disbelief.

I was left with Qasi, who gathered up his knives then ordered me in his car. I obeyed. He picked up our bikes and put them in his trunk. The car was silent except for the click of his belt.

"It wasn't me," I said unconvincingly. "I didn't know he was going to do that. I'm just as mad as you. That's why I kicked the knife out of his hand."

Qasi drove back toward the flea market. His car had a musk smell, and you could see vacuum stripes on the floor.

"So, we're going back to the flea market?" I asked.

"Yes. I've changed my mind. You are going to work for me."

"Um. OK. But I think my parents are probably going to wonder where I am."

"You probably don't care about your parents. A kid who steals doesn't care about his parents."

"I didn't steal anything."

"Right. Your accomplice did the stealing."

"I didn't steal anything."

"Do you know what would happen to you in my country if your friend did that? Do you have any idea?"

"If someone stole from a dildo salesman? No, I don't know."

Qasi stopped the car in the middle of traffic. He opened his trunk, grabbed our bikes and placed them on a tree lawn. Other motorists leered and drove slowly by, but none stopped. I didn't want to start crying. I can usually find something that can pull me out of a situation, but all I could do then was cry.

I didn't care that all the cars could see me sitting indian-style crying next to a mangled pile of bikes. I try to avoid luxuriating in my crying, but it was the only thing that felt sort of good.

* * *

Qasi drove back to the flea market and quickly packed up the contraband in his shop. Tom was going to talk about the knife and the fireworks and the sex toys. He had to get rid of all of it. First the knives, then the fireworks, then the dildos—like a three-bean salad, only with knives, fireworks and dildos. The man in the stall next to Qasi woke up while he was loading the box. He squinted and angled his head towards Qasi as if he might have a question, but then fell back asleep.

Qasi drove to the fishery and ordered frog legs from the smiling man in the paper hat who reached into the granular ice for the ribbons of amphibian flesh that held the taste of slow moving water. He looked out over Lake Erie, her green undulations pushing against the rocky pier that extolled: NO WAKE in white enamel paint. When he finished eating, he walked his box of contraband up the pier and sat at the edge. He reached his hand into the box and grabbed a fistful of dildos then flung them one at a time into the lake where they floated, bobbing with the green swells. Angry gulls flew over the sortie of dildos, pointed like missiles aimed at Canada.

§

It can take all that talk without purpose

IT WAS A JUNCO, A SHITBIRD THAT FLEW HEADFIRST into the glass wall near the entrance of the hotel. The only one to hear the short ping was the doorman, who was smoking a cigarette outside the oscillating purview of the security camera. The doorman stubbed his cigarette, walked to the bird and turned it with his boot. "Shitbird," he mumbled before he pulled his leather gloves on, then scooped it up and walked to the tree planter in front of the hotel. This tree planter—the place where he brings all birds that have flown into the glass—is also the place where the previous doorman lost his job, after he was caught having a pee behind it. The previous doorman did this every morning, as if marking his territory, only not in the way an animal does. An animal will mark his territory with urine when he's walked far enough that fear loosens his urethra. The old doorman peed because he had no fear, and this cost him his job. And, as the current doorman walks the bird over to the planter, the fact that reckoning can still occur in the shadow of a tree is a thought he will not bother himself with.

The valet, having just weathered his morning rush, is playing a video game on his cell phone when he sees the doorman standing by the planter. He walks over, holding his phone before him as if it were leading him.

"I can fix that bird," the valet tells the doorman.

"He'll wake if you just let him be," says the doorman, then looks into the sky at the long cloud that hangs low.

"My uncle knows how to fix the animals ... he taught me some things," says the valet. "He is known for this. My uncle. And he showed me some things. I can fix that bird," the valet says.

"Awright, go on and show me how to fix it," says the doorman, to which the valet puts his phone down, scoops the bird into his gloved hands and blows a steady stream of air directly into the bird's asshole.

* * *

Twenty-two floors up, Siobhan wakes. The cloud that has sluggishly plugged the sky sits one floor below her. She can see it out the large windows that line the western wall of her suite. She'd woken in the clouds. She leans up on her elbows and rests her back against the padded headboard while looking out at the cloud and the building tops that poke through.

Renting the suite was an extravagance she permitted

herself on the advice of her friend Julie, who often gave an-
noyingly expensive advice. Siobhan followed the advice because she was beginning to understand that Julie had lived
(at least married) more smartly than her; Julie's husband had
left her, but his money had not. There were so many simple
and dumb truths Siobhan felt she now must concede to. It
didn't seem fair that truths could be so stupid and coarse,
but maybe some truths also had to buy their milk at the gas
station. There was no need to think this way after sleeping in
the clouds around all this wonderful new air. Just look at how
beautiful Chicago could seem in February. This cloud sepa-
rating her from all the muck on the ground—God must be
saying something to me, Siobhan thought. Maybe God spoke
more to people who rented penthouse suites in tall hotels,
or maybe you could just hear better. And the truths here got
their milk from room service. For Siobhan the day felt light.
She slid her feet into the hotel slippers, wrapped the robe
over her shoulders then walked to one of the windows. She
looked out at the tops of the buildings, tall enough to poke
through the cloud, then at the thin reflection the window
held of her face. She remembered an old cartoon she'd seen
in which the villain somehow got his hands on a giant death
ray, and rather than obliterate continents and demand ran-
som, the villain drew a picture of his face on the moon with
it. Siobhan looked at her face imposed over the buildings and
the steam somersaulting out of their tops and understood the
impulse.

She'd spent a large portion of last night fantasizing about

eulogizing her husband. He wasn't dead. Not even close. This was not a healthy use of her time and imagination, she knew.

Siobhan's suite had a balcony blanketed in a thin layer of snow. Large icicles hung down from the roof, crowning the hotel in translucent fangs. Siobhan slid the door open then walked to the railing. Her slippered feet moved across the snow. She could hear the horns from cabs below slurring in the cold wind. She leaned over the rail to pull one of the javelin-sized icicles from the roof. It was enormous, bigger and fatter than any she'd ever held before. She lifted it above her head using both hands, which caused her robe to part. She spaced her feet out for balance under the weight, then angled the icicle into the air like it were her sword and winced out at the building tops. But the sword's momentum was more than she could bear. Her sword slapped down onto the railing and broke cleanly just above her fingers, leaving her to watch in awe as the cloud below swallowed the blade of her ice sword. She heard it hit two incredibly long seconds later, which was followed by the faint sound of a car alarm. Siobhan raised her hands to her cheeks then quickly tiptoed back into her room and sat on her bed, then rolled under the covers.

Under the covers Siobhan's fear took a poisonous turn to her ex-husband: how he'd look so hurt when she'd refuse his yearnings for isometric morning sex, refuse to commingle their dragon breaths. This would be followed by his lugubrious morning frown, more about his unheralded heroism for trying to put their stunted sex life on his back and carry it up the hill. Then she thought about her friends. She thought about her owl-like aunts gossiping over her broken marriage with their coffees. Why did she care about these things? Would she always care? Would it get worse?

Siobhan gathered her feet and sat Indian style under the duvet—this was her calming position, her reset. The room quieted. Siobhan heard the hum of something. She felt that hum wash over her body in a tingling way. She remembered sleeping at a cottage on Lake Michigan with her brother when she was young. There was a bathroom near their room and the faucet had a slow drip. Her brother in the bunk below told her that if she left that faucet go all night their hearts would mimic the pattern and kill them both while they slept. So, she got down from the top bunk and jammed a towel in the mouth of the sink.

Siobhan envisioned her ice sword dropping through the cloud. She knew then she must have speared someone, probably a mother pushing a stroller.

Minutes later there was a knock at the door, which quieted everything, even the hum. Then there was another knock.

"Engineering," came a voice from behind the door.

Siobhan heard a key slip into the door before she yelled: "Hang on a minute!"

Siobhan got out from under the duvet, tied her robe and answered the door. Outside stood a man in brown pants and white shirt with the hotel crest sewn onto it. A toolbox lay at his feet. He apologized for disturbing, then explained how ice was falling and he was there to see if he could use her balcony to prevent more from falling.

"Oh … sure. Has anyone been hurt?" Siobhan asked with a clenched face.

"No, nothing cep' a Toyota," the engineer said with a smirk.

He looked like a Bears fan, Siobhan thought, but in the best possible way. His eyes weren't caved in yet, and he had a muscular chest and arms. His teeth were big and white like his shirt. Maybe an ex-Marine. Or just a Bears fan whose body hadn't gone south yet. The engineer asked if he should come back at a better time.

"Oh no, it's OK. You can come in," she said, moving away from the door. The engineer apologized again for having disturbed her, then picked up his toolbox and waded into her suite.

"Can I get you something to drink?" Siobhan asked. "Water or juice or something, I mean."

"No thanks, Mrs. Heiyak, I'm fine," said the enginerer.

"That's not my name."

"Oh I'm sorry. I must've been looking at an old list."

"My name is Siobhan," she said.

"Oh. OK," he said with a frozen smile.

"I used to be Mrs. Heiyak."

"OK," the engineer said, then looked at the ground. "My name's Paul." His gold nametag affirmed it. He walked over to the balcony door where he looked at the giant icicles, then at the pattern on the ground that Siobhan's footprints had made.

Earlier in the week Siobhan paid a clerk at the Thompson Center to re-maiden her name. After this she ate a slice of pizza in the food court, under the piped-in sounds of Phil Collins. All the noises of the food court formed a slurry. Bored of her slice, Siobhan threw half into the snapping jaws of a trashcan then walked outside. The Thompson Center looked like an alien pod in the middle of Chicago, but it was a good thing in a city so orderly and sensible. Out front a high school choir sang gospel songs from the steps. The DeBuffet sculpture looked like a strange amalgamation of dirty snow banks that had risen and now stared at her from behind the choir. The choral voices were raw and powerful. They dove through Siobhan's body, and brought up very old tears. She tried to stop them, which made her chest heave. She put her forearm across her face as a shield then walked around the circular building to get away, but had somehow circled back to where the choir stood. She stopped and cried more as people walked quickly by without noticing her. She stayed near the steps until they finished singing and were taken away single file by two yellow buses.

Siobhan watched as Paul, the engineer, stood on her balcony speaking and shrugging into his walkie-talkie. She pretended not to stare when he turned around and walked into her suite.

"Would you mind if I used your phone?" Paul asked. "Boy, that's pretty cool how that cloud's below you like that. I've never seen anything like that." Paul walked along the side of her bed to the phone.

"I figured it just came with the room," said Siobhan.

"No that's your own, um . . . um, that's something else," Paul said, then waved his arms.

Siobhan sat by the desk in her bathrobe as Paul talked on the phone. She thought of her ex—of his body—of all the sharp places, all the chin bones and shoulder blades. Sexually, her ex-husband had devolved into a rusty playground. And he never took his socks off when they fucked. She would try to slide them off with her toes; toward the end this was the only part of intercourse that kept her intercoursing. Siobhan wanted a man with a different body, a thick body, one that had heft, like a good steak knife. She wanted better sex. Better sex beat sitting Indian style as a reset. Why had she come so late to this contemporary thinking, she wondered. She'd once read how easy it was for a woman to get a man to have sex. All you had to do was laugh at his jokes then, at some point, take his hand in yours.

Paul hung up the phone and turned around. Air was trapped in his mouth where words were held away from the ear of his supervisor. "Well it seems I won't be needin' to use your balcony," Paul said.

"Why is that?" asked Siobhan.

"I'm not supposed to touch those icicles."

"Are they poisonous?"

"According to some hotel attorney they are. If I touch those icicles the hotel can be held liable for any damage their falling causes."

"Really?"

"Yep. It's an act of God if I don't do anything," Paul said.

"An act of God if you do nothing?"

"That's right," Paul said, then picked up his toolbox and walked towards the door. "Sorry again to have bothered you."

"No, you didn't bother me," Siobhan said, walking behind him. He was leaving, Siobhan realized too late. There was nothing she could do but watch the door slowly shut then smack closed. She stood for a few seconds looking at her silhouette reflected in the laminated emergency exit instructions on the back of the door. She opened the door and peered down the corridor, where she saw Paul waiting for the elevator.

"Wait," Siobhan said, then walked out of the door in her robe.

"Mrs. Heiyak. I mean Siobhan," Paul said back then walked toward her. "What is it?"

"It wasn't an act of God. I grabbed that icicle then it broke by accident over the railing."

"I wondered if you did," Paul said, then stopped to think.

Siobhan put her hand in his and looked into his eyes. "I'm sorry. I'm such an idiot."

"What? No. No, you're not an idiot, that act of God stuff was the idiot. It was idiotic. I mean this building needs heated gutters. It's only a matter of time . . . Well, look. Let's go back to your room and I'll make a call and we can fix this," Paul said. Siobhan nodded in agreement then walked back with him to her suite.

Siobhan sat on the mattress near Paul while he called his supervisor. Paul saw her staring and smiled back at her. As he talked, Siobhan moved her gaze to the window, to the icicles and the cloud. Siobhan had the feeling of just having surfaced from somewhere deep and lightless. She felt excited about Paul being on the phone, while she sat on the bed, and the icicles were hanging outside. The whole event had taken the air of a drama that required the ordering of a pizza, the eating of it on the carpet in socks. Paul hung the phone up then announced they would have to wait as management evaluated the legal ramifications of this new wrinkle. Both Siobhan and Paul shrugged at the inefficacy of managerial dithering, but neither did more than that.

Siobhan, once again, offered Paul a drink, this time she mentioned scotch with a smile "to keep you warm when you have to go out and fight the icicles." Paul smiled but declined. He didn't drink, he explained. This created another conversational lull, which Siobhan did not want to accept. She felt a strange compulsion to make this conversation unambiguously positive. "I had the most vivid dreams last night," Siobhan said. "I mean I dream a lot usually, but the colors and the focus were more crisp, I guess, maybe it was the linens. I should buy nice linens," Siobhan continued.

"A lot of people say that," Paul remarked.

"About the linens?"

"It might be the linens. A lot of guests talk about how sharp their dreams are the next day."

"Really, the hotel should really advertise that. That's a pretty good selling advantage."

"If you have nice dreams it is. I s'pose," Paul said as Siobhan slid her hands into the robe's pockets, bending the hotel emblem over her left breast. She and Paul both had emblems stitched over their breasts.

"I dreamt about zombies," Siobhan said.

"Oh," Paul returned.

"Flesh-eating zombies. I chased them down, sometimes on motorcycles, sometimes on cigarette boats. I never ran away screaming, I always blew them away or stomped on their heads. It's a recurrent dream actually, usually not in Technicolor—like last night," Siobhan said to Paul who nodded silently. "The dream used to scare me because it was so graphic, even before the Technicolor. But I always get the zombies. I always win. I used to dream about my husband cheating on me—those dreams sucked. He never cheated on me. At least I'm pretty sure. I don't think he could have, but it doesn't really matter if he did or didn't, at least to me," Siobhan said, then took a deep breath. Paul nodded more then looked at the carpet. "Look at you nodding at the carpet, wondering why this insane woman is talking to you."

"No. You keep telling me how I feel about you. Do you usually tell people how they feel about you?

"You're not saying anything."

"Well, yeah, but that doesn't mean you can just fill stuff in. I can't remember my dreams," Paul said. "But I often wake up with the covers twisted around me and pillows laying on the floor."

"Maybe you should get yourself some nice linens."

"Maybe."

* * *

Siobhan once worked as an events organizer for an association of fire safety equipment salesmen. For hours she had to sit behind a skirted conference table passing out badges and pamphlets to ruddy-faced fire extinguisher salesmen from all over the Midwest. Part of her job involved making sure the valets returned the fire extinguisher salesmen's rented Ford Tauruses in timely fashion. During the conference two of the salesmen had somehow hooked up, maybe during cocktail hour after the dinner of pork and buttered noodles. Siobhan couldn't say, but the two fire extinguisher salesmen—one was a saleswoman—were incredibly fat. The saleswoman wore an enormous pink dress with pink pumps and thick rainbow-reflecting pantyhose that accentuated her porcine nature in an unashamed and pretty way. The salesman had a mustache and wore the same sweater that all the salesmen wore, only his was larger. They were the last two to call for their Ford Tauruses, and Siobhan remembers watching them wait. She remembers watching the woman placing her face before his, then kissing him with a heavy-breathed intensity. The saleswoman leaned her ass against the ridge of a credenza, allowing it to pour over the side. Her left pump dangled. The salesman fell into her pink vortex, their heads turned left and right. And Siobhan remembers feeling both slightly terrified and slightly aroused, but what made the scene so memorable was the lady's aggression. She'd taken such a chance.

Siobhan thought of this as she leaned into the stubbled maw of Paul and kissed him. She quickly pulled her head back to see his eyes: they'd thinned. She waited to see if he would say anything. He said nothing, so she moved back in for another. Paul cupped his hand behind her neck and they slithered across the duvet, fondling each other's new body. Siobhan unbuttoned Paul's shirt, then buried her head in his chest as if to change time and light. Siobhan inched closer to Paul's groin. The mattress quickly lost its north and south. The sheets popped in from the corners. Siobhan and Paul seldom looked at each other. Wrists, ankles and bellies asserted themselves, especially bellies. For what seemed like hours, they rubbed bellies while lightly touching the areas below with all five fingers. Twisting around on the mattress, without any overt attempt, they spun so that their faces were on top of one another. They kissed with open eyes and stopped for a moment, then Paul dropped himself into the mattress between Siobhan's raised kneecaps. Siobhan closed her eyes then opened them. She could see beyond Paul, the cloud and the building tops; she could see the icicles. She felt a gathering heat roll through her body, like a thunderstorm she'd seen while swimming in Lake Michigan, the clouds roared over the beach with a speed something as large and green as the sky should never have. Her mother was ashore yelling for her to come in. Her orgasm was like that green sky, it pulled through her as if shot from Canada. It flew out of her at a speed she thought might knock down all those icicles. She was afraid, which released more adrenaline that her body quickly relegated to her orgasm.

* * *

"'Dis bird. It is known in my village," explained the valet while pointing at the concussed bird in the planter. "It is famous for certain things. The most famous thing about dis bird . . . are you listening? It can make love to all kinds. It can hump all different types of birds, it is famous for this. Until it picks one, then it sticks with the picked one. It does not care so much about flying or making nests in the trees. It does not care about going south in the winter."

"It's not very smart," adds the doorman, who is also leering down at the fat bird.

"No. Nothing smart can fly. But dis bird, dis bird is very

famous for it can take—if you are talking, you know, just like talking to talk—it can help you understand why you are talking to talk and it can take all that talk without purpose and put it on its wings and fly it away from you."

* * *

Siobhan woke to the sound of muted voices coming from Paul's pants, which lay rolled up on the carpet. Paul was asleep. His mouth was slightly ajar, glistening at one edge. She couldn't make out what the voices were saying; it was some sort of numeric code. Maybe that was how his pants demanded to be put back on.

The fact that Paul was deep in sleep made Siobhan think he was a good man. A bad man would not be able to sleep like this. She lay still for a while, staring at the red light on the smoke alarm then across the roof to the balcony, then back to the icicles. Looking at the icicles made Siobhan feel she was sleeping on the tongue of a giant ice dog. She noticed the cloud that hung below her balcony was now gone. She could see farther down the shoulders of the buildings. She wanted to walk out onto the balcony to smoke a cigarette, but didn't want to wake Paul, whose pants were issuing muffled numbers more incessantly now. The message was for a number 3, there was a 10-1-50 in 1412.

A 10-1-50, Siobhan thought to herself. She eased off the bed, put her feet in her slippers and stood. She hadn't had sex like that in a long time. She'd forgotten how much peace it brought. She heard him shuffle around on top of the mattress; he didn't open his eyes. He turned to lay diagonal over the entire bed. Siobhan found her robe, and as she wrapped herself in it she noticed something different about her skin: it was smoother than before somehow, especially her face, which she ran her hand down. It felt downy soft. She ran her hand down her belly and legs then over her kneecap. All thick and soft.

Out on the balcony she lit a cigarette. It was cold, but all the noise was nice, her room was too quiet and warm, too womblike. That long cloud had risen about twenty feet and was now above her floor. She looked over the railing and could see the speck of a maroon Toyota whose roof had caved in, and on either side, like large jewels, sat the remnants of her ice sword. No one had bothered to cordon off the area where, even in the dead of February, there were still a lot of people walking to the shops, spas, and surgeons along Rush Street. Plastic surgery—was it still called that, Siobhan wondered. Was it like plastic explosive? With materials that were changing. Like moods. Her thoughts were interrupted by the sliding of the balcony door where Paul stood in his red boxer shorts and boots. He immediately wrapped his arms around his bare hairy chest.

"Jeezus, it's cold out here," he said at the ground.

"Where are your shirt and pants?" Siobhan said back.

"My workpants and work shirt?" Paul asked.

"Yes, your work pants and work shirt."

"I quit," Paul said.

Siobhan laughed, then pointed at Paul's feet. "Aren't those your work boots?"

Paul responded by taking the boots off. Siobhan turned away from him and leaned on the railing.

"Don't come near me," Siobhan said, unable to quell the nervous smile that was breaking across her face.

"I just want one of them icicles is all," he said.

"That's not funny," she said, turning away from him again.

"Oh. I'm sorry."

"Why has no one taped off the area below? Why haven't your people done anything?"

"They're not my people any more. I told you I quit."

"Someone could get hurt."

"Say, what happened to your cloud?"

"It moved a little higher. Not my cloud any more. I'd really like it if you put your clothes back on."

"I think we should do something about those icicles. How 'bout you? I think we should go up to where that cloud is now. I have an office up there. We can get some poles, maybe a hammer. Whaddya think?"

"Maybe I'll just wait here."

"But you should really see the view I've got up there. Now with that cloud up there, it'd be pretty amazing. 360 degrees, the lake, the smoke pumping out of every building. It might be worth it to check it out."

* * *

After much cajoling, Paul got Siobhan to follow him up to the top floor of the hotel, where there was a supply room. Siobhan followed Paul onto the roof. It was freezing cold but the view was amazing. They were near the Hancock building which looked so elegant, all alone at a cocktail party. Paul smiled at Siobhan. "On the weekend I drive up to Wisconsin and fish. I've caught sturgeon but mostly it's perch. The other days of the week I am here. I am a lucky man. And now I've met you."

Siobhan smiled, but felt nervous about what Paul might be implying.

They walked back inside, into the supply room. Paul asked Siobhan if she wanted to smoke some weed. Siobhan said no, but when Paul lit up a joint the width of a gorilla finger she couldn't help asking for a puff. She was on vacation, she reasoned, she was allowed to do things like this. It'd been a long time since she'd smoked. It made her too lethargic and hungry, but there were too many new and wild things going on for her to feel that way now, she figured. She took a small hit and held it in.

"You've done this before," Paul said, to which she blew smoke directly into his face. "I smoke a lot," Paul said. "It's not the best weed. It's cheap. You need to smoke a lot for it to do anything."

"So what's a 10-1-50?" Siobhan asked.

"A 10-1-50?"

"Yeah, what's that?"

"That means a toilet's overflowing," Paul said, exhaling.

"Oh," Siobhan said and laughed.

"The worst part of the job."

"I bet."

"Happens a lot, too. This building was built so stupidly. It's what we call a glamourpuss building."

"That sounds annoying," Siobhan said, handing Paul back the gorilla finger.

"Yeah," Paul said, and it was quiet for a little while. "Well I guess we should get back down to your room."

"We've got to defang the glamourpuss," Siobhan added.

On the elevator ride down, Paul put his hand on Siobhan's shoulder. He could actually feel her whole body stiffen then recede. He withdrew his hand. Siobhan didn't want to be touched. Paul noticed, as she exited the elevator, that something about her walk had changed, become less fluid. He was confused. He didn't know what he did to make her this way. Nothing was said about it in her room, but something had happened to her. Siobhan opened the closet for her coat but Paul told her she didn't have to go out there, that he could get the icicles off the roof. But she continued putting on her coat.

"Really, I can get 'em down," Paul said.

"No. I want to help," Siobhan said, her sentence punctuated by the whir of her jacket's zipper.

Paul shrugged, then walked outside. Siobhan followed. The wind had picked up.

"Look, you really don't need to be out here. It's cold and there's no reason."

"I want to help. Let me help."

"OK, but is everything, you know, OK?"

"Yes, well … maybe no. I don't think we should touch each other. I know that sounds stupid but I just think we shouldn't touch one another," Siobhan said back.

"OK. No touching. You know you can go back inside if you want."

"I don't want to. Please," Siobhan said, trying not to look Paul in the eye.

Paul turned around, gingerly broke an icicle off the roof and set it on the ground. He repeated this until there were four icicles lying on the floor of the balcony and the rest of the icicles were beyond his reach.

"If you need me to hold your legs I can," Siobhan said to him. "I can do that. I'm pretty sure I can do that," she said in reaction to the glance he shot her, then she crept up closer behind him.

"Look, I just freaked out for a second, but I'm fine now. Haven't you ever just freaked out for a second?" Siobhan asked, to which Paul shrugged as she picked up one of the icicles to move it out of the way. Siobhan grabbed one too. Paul angled his in his hands like it was a sword, then stared at Siobhan, who lifted her icicle up slowly, pointing it skyward before angling it with both hands across her body like a warrior. She felt a split second impulse to crack it over Paul's head, but that went away, up in the air, just like the cloud.

§

Yellow and Maroon

SEAN SLOWED THE YELLOW MOVING TRUCK NEXT TO THE curb in front of his new apartment building in Chicago. It was an old four-story red brick building with fire escapes jutting out like bent antennae, a rare feature in Chicago. He parked the truck illegally and rang the buzzer for John, his new roommate. John came down wearing a T-shirt with sunglasses hooked around the neck. He said hello and shook Sean's hand, then set the Coke down and put on his sunglasses, a subtle expression of reign over his kingdom. They didn't really know each other.

They stood there for a bit with nothing to say. It was sunny and both young men knew their lives would now change, if only maybe slightly, and this imminent change gave their day a little buoyancy. John helped Sean move a few things then explained between gulps of Coke that he had to go to a friend's house.

"What a dick," Sean said to the walking shadow of himself after John left. He couldn't imagine someone not helping and still being a decent guy.

It was a fourth-floor walkup, so he figured he'd move in two waves so his stuff wouldn't get ripped off. While lifting his bedframe, a Mexican guy with a mesh-backed Chicago Refrigeration hat hopped on the back of the truck and waved, then started lifting things out and up to the landing. The Mexican spoke broken English, but communicated through nodding and smiling.

This was something someone who had never before lived in a city would allow: nonemergency volunteerism. During one wave Sean stepped onto the truck to see the Mexican lining up cocaine that looked like it had come out of a butter wrapper on his dresser. Sean picked up a crate of records, figuring it best to ignore the defiling of his furniture.

"Amigo!" the Mexican shouted, then waved from the dark recess of the truck, his hand like the belly of a hooked fish flitting near the surface of the water. Sean had never tried the stuff. But he'd left Ohio. He was allowed to try this, he thought. His family was involved in politics, so these decisions always involved more than him, but that was in Ohio. And what chance would there be that this situation would repeat itself?

It's amazing how quickly the rest of the move went, like one of those sped-up Benny Hill chases that, as a kid, Sean stayed up to watch for the slight chance to glimpse a pair of boobs; it was cruel that you had to wade through the unfunny Benny Hill for this. He asked the Mexican if he wanted to have a beer with him once they'd finished, but the Mexican politely refused. He reached in his pocket to give him some money and came up with $27, which he handed over. "I'm not a rich man," Sean said, to which the Mexican nodded and smiled full-tooth, taking the money and handing Sean a card with his name and number on it.

"Not yet," the guy said. "Maybe I help you become rich man."

There was a pause as Sean started to register what he was saying. "You give me a call, if you or your friends need stuff."

Sean looked at the card, nodded and said, "OK," while offering a hand to shake.

The door to the apartment opened into the kitchen. The kitchen had a window with a direct view of the Hancock Building. It was near dusk and the late sun striated the skyline with maroons into golds into pale blues: beautiful yet lonely. It was hypnotic and made him giddy, but also a little terrified. Sean's space was just off to the right. The windows had maroon moldings that faced west like open mouths. The walls and wood floors were shabbily painted a dry dandelion yellow. Sean walked around his room, alone with the creaking of the wood. He looked out the windows in the front and saw the Mexican walking down a road that led to a church with two bell towers rolled in chicken wire. Sean pulled out the Mexican's business card and threw it in the trash, then plopped down on his couch and fell asleep.

* * *

Sean was surprised when the Field Museum called to say he'd been hired. He interviewed thinking it just more an excuse to visit the city. He knew his family could find him a job, but he wanted to earn one on his own. Unlike most people who study horses, his family didn't own any or even have a barn. They were Clevelanders. The closest they'd gotten to horses was at the church race night, where they bet on lurching metal statuettes while his dad glad-handed parishioners eating glazed donuts with coffee.

His family was nonplussed with this horse obsession, even found it disturbingly feminine. They were there with Sean at the National Gallery in London when the obsession took root. They were taking in the sights together before dropping him off in the exchange program. He was transfixed before the life-size painting of the colt Whistlejacket by George Stubbs: the chestnut coat flowing over muscle and bone to the face, and that eye that seemed to apologize for a strength it couldn't fully control. His eyes, nose and ears were all large and panoramic; he was prey, over one thousand pounds of prey with thin legs that could shoot him through fields. Sean felt he'd dreamt about the painting before he'd seen it. The animal was so beautiful and strong and so afraid.

But his attraction to horses didn't make him want to necessarily be near the animal, just near the idea of the animal. He worked at a thoroughbred farm in England mucking stalls mostly, but it didn't do as much for him as the painting. And that's why the Field Museum job was perfect. They were mounting an exhibit, *The Horse*, and the scientists involved were making big discoveries about when man began domesticating the horse, and what it meant for the animal. What it got in return for agreeing to work with humans.

* * *

There was a time when Sean thought about entering politics like his father, but that changed one election night when he was thirteen. He woke up at 4:00 a.m. All the Knights of Columbus candy he'd eaten at the different re-elect triages had bitten into his stomach. He got out of bed to get himself some milk. At the fridge, Sean saw his father sitting alone in the darkened family room with the TV off, wearing his slackened suit. He'd won the election; it wasn't even close. The first thing Sean thought of was a classmate who told him he woke up late one night to find his dad watching porn in the family room. Sean's father looked over at him in the refrigerator light and patted the couch next to him. Sean walked the carton of milk over to the couch. His dad stared at him.

"Aren't you happy you won, Dad?"

"I don't know. Are you?"

Sean shrugged and took a gulp of milk.

"I should be happy, right?"

Sean nodded yes.

"So why don't I just be happy then, right?"

* * *

Sean woke from his nap to summer darkness. It was almost one in the morning, and he was incredibly sore and sunburned. His body felt cased in something too small. But it felt good to be sore. He tried not to trip over the boxes, using the orange-yellow sulfur light of the street lamps to guide him to the bathroom and kitchen. On the table there was a postcard invite to a party and a sea monkey with a note under it that read "Housewarming Present." Sean found a glass and filled it with water, then dropped the sea monkey in and waited for the peach flesh to swell.

It reminded him of his brother Kyle sitting in the kitchen after school with swollen fists dipped in glasses of water. Kyle was always hurling kids into pricker bushes, fish-hooking them before a crowd of bored or bloodthirsty cross-armed boys. He found some sort of reason for violence, and it wasn't just some phase he grew out of. He never laid a hand on Sean, even when Sean tried roughhousing with him. Kyle would just laugh and find some sort of leveraged position so he could

hold him back and laugh more. Sean never had to fight anyone in grade school. Kyle had blazed a trail, relieving him of
any obligation to uphold valor. It was better for Kyle to stay
home and be the politician, Sean thought.

The party was at a warehouse on Lake Street. Sean drove
the hollowed-out van there. Maybe he would make a bunch
of friends, throw them in the back, slap down the buckle and
bring them to his apartment where he could take a picture of
them and send it to his parents to assuage what seemed to be
their only worry about his move. Why did he want to be alone?

He was growing weary of his college friends. They had
grown apart. They treated school like it was a vacation from
the unavoidability of their preconfigured lives; they were
friends with him for his family's connections, nothing else. It
had always been obvious and he was too lazy to ignore their
friending efforts. It's OK for a friendship to start that way, but
it went nowhere else; there was no discovery.

The first floor of the party was filled with empty oil
drums that people were banging on with sticks. There was an
ottoman in the middle of the room that had more sticks if you
wanted to join the session. Past this there was a kitchen. In
one corner people were dancing to mambo records playing
on a suitcase record player. It was a lot better than any party
he'd ever been to, and not knowing anyone there wasn't annoying. It was the reason he chose Chicago over places like
New York where your cadre of friends was like your bulwark

against an ugly world, and you weren't going to take chances adding anyone you didn't know. Upstairs was the dance floor, and it wasn't long before Sean spotted his roommate John on the floor. John was happy to see him, even hugged him, which felt good, this bunching of his sore shoulders and muscles. John walked him around, introducing him to everyone he knew, which was over half the room. The introductions were quick and a little embarrassing, but it was nice for Sean to see John make the effort. Unfortunately, no small talk caught. Rather than drink too much he decided to head down to the oil drums. Drumming might help with his sore shoulders, he thought.

After drumming for a bit Sean sat down against a wall in the room with all the oil drums and closed his eyes, letting the tempo overcome everything. The trip and the move had taken more out of him than he realized. He quickly fell asleep, a cup of beer in his hand. He dreamt he was on a boat slipping down a river. He had a rifle and a coat with fringe on it, and from the wooded banks, life-size cardboard pictures of bears and Indians would pop up and he would shoot at them. Someone at the party tapped his leg and he woke.

"You OK, Holmes?"

"Yeah. Thanks."

"No problem. Wasn't sure if you were breathing, yo. Wanna see something crazy?"

"Um, OK."

The guy who woke Sean was a little older. He was skinny, smoking a cigarette, looked a little wiry and off, like one of those roasted looking characters who troll around town on a stolen mountain bike. He had Sean follow him outside through a corridor into what looked like another warehouse. Sean recognized the earthy smells from this warehouse, and seeing the tack wall confirmed that he was in a stable. Empty carriages fronted with a placard that read The Wabash Horse filled most of the stalls. The strange guy walked him over to the paddock where a few people were standing, drinking beer and looking at a draft horse that seemed mildly interested in them.

"It seems like a cruel thing to me," a woman was saying.

"I say we set 'em free," a guy said and laughed.

Sean wandered over to the roan standing in his stall and pet him on his nose. Usually the white horses have only gray or black in them, but this guy had red. He bent his long head down into the cup of beer Sean was holding and plashed his fat tongue into it. Something about seeing a flash of horse teeth destroys their elegance; maybe this is why Asian women cover their mouths when they laugh.

Sean heard a guy behind him say, "That dude just gave the horse beer," and start laughing. Beer was good for horses.

It helped them keep their appetites up and calmed them. The woman he was with did not laugh, walked over to him and asked him if he gave the roan beer. He did, he explained. "They like it."

"That's fucked up," the woman said.

"No, they like it, really. It's not all that bad for them."

"No. That's fucked up," she repeated.

One of the men she was with, a short bald guy with broad shoulders you could see through his tank top, and lateral muscles arched and layered under a button down shirt said, "Maybe it's OK, maybe he knows about this, baby."

"White boys from all over are moving into this neighborhood," another man said, and laughed. Sean looked at the woman and explained that he knew a lot about horses and he wasn't trying to hurt it.

"This horse is good around people," he told her, then pet its head and stroked its ears. "He likes the attention."

"He the Lone Ranger," the bald guy said.

Why is this the only horse in the stable? Sean thought. It was cruel to leave him all alone. He needed friends. What Sean or the others didn't see or smell yet was a smoldering fire that was growing behind one of the carriages in the back of the stable, where someone must have tossed a cigarette. The roan noticed and was the first to look agitated, flashing the whites of his eyes. The smell seemed to hit everyone at the same time. The fire alarm went off, but the sprinkler heads did nothing. Everyone but the girl, her boyfriend and Sean ran out of the barn. The smoke was coming from behind a wall they couldn't get to. The roan had no halter or bridle on, and with his agitation magnifying there would be no way to get either on him.

Sean told the couple to get out, that he would get the horse out but that they needed to leave or risk getting kicked. They left. Sean unlocked the stall, and with the roan now rearing, ran around the stable not sure how to get the roan out. This seemed to stir the fire and the smoke. Sean tried to grab the horse around the neck. Someone propped the door open, stoking the fire with fresh oxygen. Sean grabbed a halter and tried not to panic, but the halter was not going to work. He raised his hands before the horse, then grabbed it by its ear; the roan submitted.

There was enough smoke and commotion that people had assembled outside the stable. The sprinklers were now on and wherever the fire was, it seemed defeated. John was in the crowd watching, Solo cup in hand. The sound of police sirens would eventually disperse them, but before that, the revelers were afforded a timeless spectacle: Sean, like Lady Godiva, lowering his head next to the roan's while riding it without saddle or reins out of the smoldering stable's back door. At first, people seemed stunned as the white horse milled through them with Sean on its back. And this was how Sean officially became a Chicagoan, though this moment of triumph or relief would be short-lived. Once the sirens came into earshot, the people scattered, spooking the roan, which threw Sean into the street and cantered down Halsted.

John ran over to help. Once Sean's wind returned, he explained that they needed to catch the roan. The moving van was two streets away. The roan wouldn't get very far, but the number of obstacles put him in serious danger. They ran for the truck, fortuitously parked in the direction the roan was cantering.

In the cab, John was pretty drunk but smiling, still amazed by the sight of his new roommate emerging on horseback from a burning stable. The roan was not in sight as the empty truck bounced onto Halsted; there were some prostitutes near the bridge that might be able to help. They rolled up and asked if they'd seen a horse, but they just stared at them trying to figure out what they were saying. You want some white horse baby?

John thought the roan might try to go somewhere quiet and grassy, but horses weren't like that. More likely, it would run itself ragged and end up wherever that took him. Hopefully without breaking a leg. Horses are good at breaking their legs. Thinking the prostitutes would have known what they were talking about if they'd seen the roan, they turned around and tried side streets. It would be a miracle if the horse was still standing, with all the cars and pocked streets. Sean felt sick at realizing this mission was migrating from rescuing the horse to making sure it was quickly put down. He was witness to this awful rite in England when he worked on that small thoroughbred farm. A filly had broken her leg in a hole. The calm doctor parted the sea of workers with an oversized syringe filled with bright pink liquid. A horse has to be able to hold itself up.

John asked if Sean was OK, reminding him that he took a pretty big fall. But Sean's body was beyond the point of accurately communicating any problems. He was taught how to get thrown from a horse. The big thing was making sure you weren't stepped on. You had to fall away from the horse. Luckily Sean found a way to bruise all parts of his back equally. It would hurt to walk for the next couple weeks, but if they found the roan it would be something he could be proud of. It definitely changed the dynamic with John, who had seemed intent on establishing his alpha role, but now sat wide-eyed, ready to follow through any plan Sean might come up with to capture the horse. They turned down a side street. Sean didn't see the speed hump in it and bounded over it. It was enough to send John's stomach up and his head out the window to unleash a sour mix of half digested Pabst Blue Ribbon and macaroni and cheese. Sean apologized, but John seemed relieved, almost thankful, for the maneuver which freed him from the hipster stew that burbled in his stomach.

"I think it's going to be fun living with you," John said, and stopped to look at Sean in a way that made him seem truly happy and somewhat vulnerable.

"I'm sure every night will be just like this," Sean said then rolled down his window all the way. The moment was broken by the shouts of women. The prostitutes. Sean turned the empty vessel around and made his way back to their corner. They were waving at him.

"We seen your white horse," a painted one with trampled flesh yelled. She didn't have to say anything else. The roan was just ahead of them and seemed to be going at a natural trot, as if for a light morning jog. It probably walked this route daily, Sean thought. Sean rode up alongside the roan, which seemed unaffected by him or the truck. They were drawing near a red light. Sean stepped on it, aiming to get the van into the intersection and direct the cars with the green to stop. Not a good thing to be doing at 2:00 a.m. in this neighborhood. As he crept into the intersection, he could see a string of headlights growing brighter and bigger. They weren't slowing. He looked in his mirror and, to his shock, saw the roan stopped and waiting at the red light. He steered the van into the median and walked back to the roan, who didn't seem all that unhappy to see him.

Sean created a makeshift halter out of rope and walked the roan back to the stable, where his owner came rushing over and hugged the mare. Both the fire and the party had been extinguished. A pair of policemen followed the owner; one gave the roan an apple.

"Were you the one that got him out of the stable?" the other cop asked.

Sean beamed. "Yes." Only in hindsight would this seem the wrong thing to say.

From the cab of the moving van, now parallel parked just ahead of the roan's homecoming ceremony, John watched as his new roommate was escorted into a police cruiser.

* * *

Sean was left alone in the back of the cop car for a while with nothing but the radio listing off all the bad things going on around town in numeric code. His new roommate John had crept alongside the cruiser in the moving van. He had a kind of smirk, and was waving to him. He mouthed that he'd bring the van home, then flashed a peace symbol and took off.

The police would do nothing but keep Sean from his new life for a few hours. There was nothing all that interesting about his story and nothing rewarding about booking him. The cops seemed disappointed by how boring his life and circumstances were. They had a laugh about the horse and this Ohio boy that rode it, got dumped by it, then rescued it.

"Why would you save a horse that threw you to the ground? People don't do shit like that here," one cop said at him so the rest would laugh.

The sky was a royal blue, a mixture of streetlamps and sunrise. The sun came up earlier here, and you didn't watch the sun set from the beaches of Chicago, you watched it rise. The grid of streets allowed Sean to walk home using just three streets, not having to think about directions. His body had stored the soreness from the day and was no longer holding anything back. It flooded through his back and shoulders. If only he could molt this skin and leave it in some gas station restroom like an enormous French tickler.

The moving van was parked illegally, the keys still glittering in the ignition. Sean grabbed the keys then made his way up the steps to his apartment. He could hear hip-hop pulsing through the stairway as he neared the landing. The door led into the kitchen where a small group was gathered. His section of the apartment was off to the right. As he made his way to his couch people turned and pointed. One guy started clapping and said his name. Another came up to him with a cocked arm ready to do one of those slap shakes. He obliged and they led him into John's part of the apartment, which was much larger, with mosaic tile roughly set into the floor around painted wood planks. His windows looked into the now glowing loop that looked like a dying campfire. The lights were off and someone was projecting a video onto a bed sheet that hung from the rafters.

"Yo, back it up. He's here," someone yelled. John came over and gave him another hug. Sean recognized the video on the sheet was shot the night of the party. They were fast-forwarding it to the scene outside the stable. They started playing it just before he came out of the stable on the roan and everyone screamed and a few clapped for him as Sean watched himself on the bed sheet ride the horse out of the stable. Someone handed him a glass that smelled like gin and tonic. He sat down on a couch, not knowing what to do with everyone's attention. Across from him sat a girl in a dress sitting with her legs far apart to reveal maroon underpants. She kind of squinted at him and he sort of shrugged which made her laugh and whisper something to her friend. Sean wondered what was going to eventually happen when he had to talk to someone. Maybe it was better never to talk to anyone. The DJ in the corner had his shirt off and started to play a disco record. People looked over at him and he held up the gatefold, which was a picture of a voluptuous woman pouring honey down her body. It was the Ohio Players, and it was unclear if this was chosen in his honor. It made Sean uncomfortable, as if it all were some sort of trap. If he allowed himself this pleasure it would only come back to hurt him. Everyone but the girl with the maroon underthings across from him got up to dance. She'd since closed her legs more and ran her hand over her kneecap, then stuck her tongue out at him, which made him laugh and look at the ground. She got up, walked over to him and asked for his hand. Sean explained that he was a terrible dancer, but she just kept her hand out. He took it and walked with her, but she walked him past the dance floor through the kitchen and into his room, closing the door. She kept leading him through the boxes to one that was open. Inside was an adult novelty gift his friends had gotten him as a going away present. It was a blow-up sheep with a bunghole that he remembers his friend using to hold a can of beer at his going away party. He distinctly remembered not packing the sheep, but somehow here it was.

"What the fuck is that?" the girl asked.

"Um . . . that. That was my going away present."

"Where were you leaving?"

"Ohio."

"Ohio sounds pretty fucked up."

"It is, but that's not why. That's just a joke. Were you going through my things?"

The girl shrugged. "Your old friends are pretty messed up. Did you all get together and fuck that thing?"

"Yeah, of course. That's what you do in Ohio."

"OK, then," she said, sensing that she was no longer welcome. She opened the door to leave, but looked back for him to say something, a correction of tone that might keep her there. But he wanted her to leave. He wanted to be alone. He wasn't tired any more. He was a little disgusted with all these people trying to make something out of him. His whole life he had watched his father manipulating this sort of falseness. It had power over him and it was stupid. Maybe it took a different kind of humility or optimism to not despise the momentum of crowds.

He'd forgotten the first thing you have to do when you move is set up your bed. His couch might have worked. All the different shaped boxes lined up looked like a miniature city. Muted sunlight was crawling through the windows and carving out the avenues his boxes made. His city. He walked into his bedroom to set up his bed. But it was already put together with sheets and everything, there was also a girl passed out on top of the duvet and near her booted feet, a FedEx envelope addressed to him.

Sean sat at the end of his bed that had somehow put itself together and attracted a drunk female, and opened the envelope to find a check and a handwritten letter from his father.

Dear Sean,
I'm so proud of you. I think it's great that you've decided to see what Chicago holds for you. I have no doubt you will succeed at the Field Museum. You will inspire others and they will inspire you. You've always been courageous and independent, since the day you were born. I wish you the best. But I want you to remember that your family is here and in the end, it's the most

important thing you have. You will come to understand this, and I just want that to happen sooner rather than later. Years slip by, but you can't let your family slip by. Your place is here and it will always be here. I love you, son, and I want you to explore. I'm going to keep this short. I want you to have a little money to get started, maybe take your roommate out to dinner. Sometimes a $50 dinner can pay remarkable dividends. I know you say you're no good at "smiling through it," but you'd be surprised what you find out about yourself when you have dinner with someone else. And sometimes you have to smile through it; you'll also learn that maybe sooner or maybe later. I hope sooner. You are principled, always have been and you protect these principles when maybe you need to let them loose and test them. You have to let them breathe. Your family is always here for you.

Love,
Dad

Sean laid the letter on his bed and stared at the arc of the handwriting. He can't remember the last time he'd read a handwritten letter from his dad. The cursive had tight loops and arcs. It was amazing how it conveyed the person. The moment was interrupted by small snoring noises from the girl lying on his bed. Sean carefully turned her on her side. She had full cheeks and a sweet Michigan toughness to her. He unlaced her boots and slipped them off and listened to her breathe for a little while. He folded the letter and picked up the check and walked to his living room. As he passed the waste basket he saw the business card the cocaine man gave him earlier. He thought about ripping up the check and tossing it on top, but it was a lot of money.

§

Driftless

THE HANDSOME MAN WHO OPENED A SHOP THAT SOLD
espresso for people to sip as they have their European motorcycles repaired snaked through the line of bikes. Steam from
his espresso vapored his big stubbled smile as he descended
upon his customers. They were the reverse of the more com-
mon overworked executive who buys a Harley and spends
more time cleaning the chrome than riding. The man knew
a lot of people bought motorcycles to assert some identity, so
curating that projection was part of his service. The shop was
down the street from me and had a mechanic who knew my
bike well. And the espresso wasn't bad, so I looked past my
grievance at this marketing fatuousness.

The handsome man, knowing it was wise to compliment
his customers' bikes, stopped by mine and started chatting
up my BMW. I proudly accepted the compliments about
equipment decisions I hadn't made (the raised bars, the crash
guards). I told him I was taking it to the Driftless Region in
Wisconsin to do some fishing. He gave a squinty nod to as-

sure me I was one of the authentic ones, then warned about
the perils of riding down desolate runs with no cell transmis-
sion, of bleeding out next to a cornfield. He placed his hand
on my shoulder. I stared at his hand, then at him. He smiled.

* * *

The Driftless Region stretches across Wisconsin and Iowa, the
slab of Midwest untouched by the rolling pin of the glaciers.
The exotic topography made streams and rivers possible. It
brought trout, and that's what brought me.

I bought the bike from an old hippy who had it in Colo-
rado. It'd been ridden hard and hadn't been kept up all that
well, but it was a BMW so it wasn't as prone as say, a British
bike with overcomplicated engineering. It had a Rotax engine, which was considered bombproof.

I rode it around the backside of my house so I could outfit
it in the shade. I had to mount the cases and figure out the
best way to get my gear in. Waders, boots, fly boxes, rods, reels,
tools in case of a flat or break down. I whittled it down as best
I could. My wife was learning Portuguese through insipid hip-
hop. I could hear her rapping with bravado through a window.

It's a four and a half hour ride across Rockford and up the
early-spring tannish-brown underbelly of Wisconsin, breaking
west at Madison. Unlike other major cities, there's really nothing around Chicago but exurbs that spread over the flat land

like spilled coffee.

* * *

I was beginning to think of my marriage like this. We'd ignored the bland periphery until we found ourselves surrounded in a dark wood. No one was to blame for the contempt we found in things, like the way we melted butter in a pan. It wasn't that we were afraid of going after any underpinning reasons, we just couldn't find them. And it's very bad not being able to find them. A lot of our friends' marriages were collapsing under the weight of phantom opportunity cost. We felt bad for these couples; they seemed blindsided by one person freaking out about squandering a life. Maybe there was more to it that we couldn't see. These crumbling marriages at first had a galvanizing effect, but that sort of energy doesn't last, and it can have an ugly tail that whips around, until eventually you see an inevitability rolling forward.

It's mostly brown trout in the river, but there are also some brooks and rainbows. A lot of the rivers are catch and release, which is fine. I didn't need to keep the fish. You gradually become a part of the river as the birds stitch across the banks, the insects hatch and the wide lip bubbles pulse across the surface. I get lost in these rivers. One time I came out into a field of mares. I think they were quarter horses. Their hinds were muscled and their front legs were kind of stubby. They were grazing in the soft afternoon sun. I walked through the grid of legs and one followed me. I tried not to make eye contact but it was impossible; it was like she was waiting for me. The mare followed me to the end of the field, hoping for me to explain myself. She wanted me to pet her, so I let the warm air from her comma-shaped nostrils pour over me and listened to the air move in and out of her gigantic lungs.

* * *

I've been chased by bulls, and stood my ground as the indifferent dairy cows swept through a field pulling the grass out of the earth with their maws. The black bulls, the all-beefs— they're different. They're ready to fight if you cross their territory. This mare just wanted to know who I was. Maybe she felt she was different from the others.

My wife packed a sandwich for me. I was a little surprised by this. She'd never really seemed to want the role of mother or wife. If it wasn't for her family, maybe she wouldn't have even thought she needed to be married. She's career-minded, smarter and better connected than me, but I make a lot of money, and maybe that helps me keep her. My job isn't all that complicated. I've taken advantage of my superiors' warranted fears of algorithms and technology. I work for an insurance company, but I don't really have anything to do with insurance. I deal with currencies. By law, an insurance company has to hold money in reserve so it can pay off its policies. For whatever reason they don't stipulate the currency, which allows me to game the currency markets, buying and selling, opening a new "revenue stream." There's no fee for moving money like this. Banks have dug this pig trail and combed it with the wide foreheads of their lobbyists. What I do isn't hard, and I don't have to like the people I work with. Some people really have to at least pretend that they like everyone. My boss once explained he's never faking it when he deals with a client, he's temporarily forgetting how much he hates them. There's a big difference. You can't fake it, he said.

It was still dark out and a little colder than I'd wanted it to be. I had a heated vest and gloves that plugged into the bike, but four hours is a long time to fight a cold that wants to crawl into everything. The sky was starting to purple and the empty highway pooled the yellow orange light from the sodium lamps. Heading through Illinois, all of the trees, the plants, everything is planted neatly in rows. Nothing is wild— feral maybe, but not wild. Maybe the prairie was too easy to tear apart or its beauty too sublime; somehow this penchant to organize and own took. No part of the landscape could escape intent. I would need to think about other things to stay awake. I never had this problem, but I was hearing the engine in clips, like I was missing a few seconds of consciousness every now and then. I turned down my heated vest and throttled up a bit.

The sun was coming up as I rolled through Rockford. The corrugated warehouses along the side of the highway looked like giant sheet cakes lying in the grass waiting to be sliced. My mind wandered but not very far. I thought about my wife in bed, and the cat pawing the covers on top of her, and the song for an advertisement for Cotton Club. Luckily it wasn't too much further. I planned on eating the sandwich my wife packed on the bank of the Kickapoo River. I hoped the day would catch up and stop feeling strange.

It was slightly overcast with the sun unwilling to burn through. It was the perfect day to fish. I looked over my patterns as I ate. I wanted to use the stonefly because it had a little heft and was easier to cast in the wider parts of the river. I dipped my boot into the water and grabbed a rock so I could see what sort of larvae squirmed underneath; this is what the fish would expect to eat, and how I would chose what fly to use. I walked down to the first pool and started working the water. I had a strike right away and was able to set the hook. It was a brown trout about a foot long. No trophy, but he had a good amount of fight, so I let him run three times. I try not to draw this out. I've watched too many people exaggerate it, but he might have snapped my line if I didn't let him have his terms. The muted sun hit his spots in a way that brought out dense reds and greens, like jumping jacks spinning in your hands.

Trout can't be out of the water too long, so I was quick to dispatch this guy. Rednecks can hold their channel cats out for hours, letting everyone in the village ogle their pink quarry, but trout won't last. He was croaking loudly at me. This was a new thing, maybe it was from the cold winter we had.

It was a relief to get the first fish. The feeling of doom and divine abandonment abate and you open to the possibilities

Driftless

of having a great day. I brought a flask of nice rye with me and even though it wasn't quite 10:00 a.m., I'd earned a hork. Just enough to warm the feet without clouding the head. I worked about a half mile of the water before taking a break. I caught a few brook trout and a largemouth bass. Nothing all that sizeable, but I don't care about that. The bigger the fish, the more moldering. I snapped a picture of one of the brooks I caught and sent it to my wife, then ate some more of the sandwich she made for me. The Kickapoo was big and wide; it was always the first stop. As the day wore on I picked smaller, denser streams. More difficult and less charted.

* * *

There was a car parked near my bike. As I rode out, I saw its passengers' belay lines hanging from the top of a cliff. They were about halfway up. I listened to their voices and their shuffling feet. It felt nice to be back on the bike, with a curtain of dirt trailing me. I had only gone a couple of miles before I came upon another fisherman who was in the road, bending down to pick something up. He jumped up when he saw me and ran right into the path I'd veered in to get away from him. I'm pretty sure I jumped off the bike before it hit the ground, but I'm not positive. I'd always wondered what my body would do if I were to crash. Would I instinctively make the right move? I rolled to the side of the dirt road into a ditch. It didn't hurt at all, and I had so much gear on that I didn't even scrape a knee, my waders appeared sound. The guy I hit was lying on the ground about ten feet away. I remember the quiet just before I pulled my helmet off, then looked at my bike lying in the reeds, as if drunkenly napping. The handlebars were bent.

The guy I hit was sitting in the road. I walked over to him and asked if he was OK, but I was in a daze. I wasn't able to do anything but ask that and stare at him. I must have hit my head. I could feel an abrasion above my left temple. The guy had dark hair, dark eyes and skin the color of pale tea. He looked Middle Eastern. He was staring beyond me into the sky and his lips were moving. He was chanting something. I stood by him and looked out over the undulating grassy hills while he looked at the sky. He would chant something at me then I'd say, "Are you O.K.?" Then he'd chant something at me and I'd ask, "Are you O.K.?" After a while he tried to stand up, and I cautioned him to take it slow. He got to his feet, looked at me with a strange expression, took a step, then fell. I was able to grab his coat, and caught him with his head suspended over a flat piece of limestone.

The cell reception was spotty, and we were in one of the dead spots. I didn't know the extent of damage to him, but could feel the bike ride through a solid body; it wasn't a glancing blow. One of his legs wasn't working right and the other had a nice gash that maybe the heat from the crash helped cauterize, but it still needed to be bandaged. I offered my shirt, but he wasn't having it. He said his car was just down the road and had better supplies if I could help him to it. He pointed to a bump on my head and wondered if I was all right.

I ran my finger over the lump on my forehead. I was scared by the fact that my adrenaline had masked whatever pain I was supposed to feel. I began to feel different thoughts and emotions course through my head, the way they do when you're falling asleep. I sat down next to the man I hit and waited for my head to gather. I asked him what he was chanting.

His name was Medhi. And he didn't know what he was chanting, so I tried to repeat it back to him. He threw me a strange look. We needed to get him some help. I tried chanting louder so he could tell me what it meant. My mind wasn't focusing on the proper things. He explained his car wasn't far away, and if I helped him get there we could repair our injuries. His one leg still worked, so I was able to sling him over me. He wasn't very big.

* * *

Most fishermen see immigrants as primal threats to their land; I don't like this about most fishermen. And being from the Middle East was probably frowned on more than the usual leers the Poles and Hispanics get. It took courage for this guy to be out here, and I respected that. It was quiet for a little while; our bodies adjusted to one another and we found a rhythm. I asked Medhi if his father taught him to fish, and he explained that he had taught himself. Everyone I know learned to fish from their dad. He filled the silence by explaining he traveled a lot after college and fell in love with an Irish girl who studied in France with him. Her family didn't like that he was Persian, but he was able to get a fishing trip with her father.

"The Irish will give you a chance," he explained. "Iranians are the same way." But, he went on to explain, if he was going to ingratiate himself with her family, he would have to learn to fish, and he would need to understand all the rules and techniques. There was a ledger his girlfriend's family kept for the river that crossed their property. It went back to the 1890s. There were so many rules, but he knew any effort on his part would impress her father. He needed to be able to cast confidently without spooking any of the fish, and timing was important; you can't loop blindly. They don't stock fish. What you caught was wild, and wild fish spook at footsteps and strange slants of light.

"Did you catch anything?" I asked.

"What, today?"

"No. In Ireland. With her father."

"I did. But that didn't matter as much as knowing what I was doing and showing that I understood. Anyone can catch a fish."

"Did you ingratiate yourself with her father?"

"I did, but she liked me more when her dad hated me."

"How does your leg feel?"

"Not too bad yet. It will hurt more soon." As Medhi answered, my cell phone rang. It was my wife. I could tell by the ring.

"We've walked into a live spot," I explained. But Medhi averted his eyes, as if he didn't really care. I stopped and he shot me a look.

"Why don't we sit over there and I'll call for the ambulance?"

"But we're not very far now."

"Far from what?"

"Far from my car."

"What are you talking about? One leg is broken and the other is gashed."

"Not broken. Just a sprain."

"Are you shitting me?"

"It's not that bad. I don't need an ambulance," Medhi said, and it was quiet for a while.

"Look, you need someone to take you to the hospital."

"I'm fine. We're almost there. If you can just bring me to my car, then it will all be over. You won't be responsible for my injuries."

"I'm not worried about that."

"We're not far," he repeated.

"I'm calling an ambulance."

"No. No. It's not necessary."

"The fuck it's not. There's no need to be a tough guy here."

"Please. No ambulance. You won't owe me anything."

"What's going on here?"

"It's just that we're not far from my car. Why waste emergency resources. If you can just get me to my car, like I said, you will bear no responsibility."

You'd think someone like me who worked in insurance would insure, at least to the legal requirement, his vehicles. I did not. I can't remember if it was some sort of rebuke of the industry or if I just forgot to mail some form. If he got me for hitting him, it could push me into bankruptcy. I didn't have $40,000 or whatever lying around. And for this asshole bending to pick up a nickel in the middle of the fucking road? He'd tell someone. They'd google "soft tissue damage," then lawyer up.

But this didn't matter because Medhi didn't want an ambulance. Maybe he was illegal. I wondered about my bike and how bad it was. I could probably bend the bars back. It was bombproof. Maybe we could both continue on like nothing happened, just a little bent up. No need to call in the authorities. I could get him to his car and he could go home and get back to making his fertilizer bomb or whatever the fuck it was he was doing that made him afraid to go to a hospital, and I could ride back to my wife with a story about my success on the river. There'd be a side story about a Persian guy I nearly flattened, but just a side note, like a bunch of mares near the road.

"Was that your wife on the phone?" Medhi asked.

"Yeah."

"It's funny how they know when something happens."

"What do you mean?" I asked.

"Does she usually call you when you're fishing?"

"I guess not. Actually, I should see why she called."

"She called to see if you were OK."

"How do you know?"

"They know when something happens."

"Can you do me a favor?" Medhi asked.

"What?"

"Can you repeat what I was chanting again?"

I repeated the chant; somehow I remembered it. Medhi smiled, and I decided not to ask him why.

If we kept walking it wouldn't be long until we were out of range again. It was possible Medhi would come to his senses when the adrenaline wore off and ask me to call an ambulance. It was equally possible he would pass out before we got to wherever it is we were supposed to be going.

As we walked together, we talked less but it didn't feel uncomfortable. Our movements grew more in sync; we were beginning to unconsciously understand and trust one another physically, like we were becoming one person.

* * *

I shut my mind off but an image fell in: a raw hamburger spinning in a microwave. It was during a sleepover; a friend and I had just made amends after a fistfight earlier in the week. Microwaves were recently deployed to the suburbs, and people still thought you could actually cook food in them. It was after supper but I'd missed the meal at home, so my friend put a raw hamburger patty in the microwave for me; we watched it spin and exude blood and rainbow-flecked bubbles. We cooked it for seven minutes but it never turned a hamburger color. Earlier that week, we had fought. An after-school brawl with spectators. We were in the park near a shelter of picnic tables and our classmates were discussing how we could tell who won the fight. Blood? Broken bone? Nothing was agreed upon before we started. I was a little smarter than him and knew more about leverage. I was also a little bigger. I got him to the ground early. But I just stared at him and let him shake it off. After he shook it off, he knew that he could beat me. That I didn't have it in me to take him out. I felt a little shame about this.

Would I also let this stranger, this immigrant, get up and walk over me?

"How is your head?" Medhi asked.

"It's fine. Better than your leg."

"My leg isn't bad. I guess I'm lucky you're helping me. A lot of fishermen would have taken off."

"Naw."

"No. They probably wouldn't stop for a … what is it … a sand nigger?" Medhi looked at me and laughed. "You're uncomfortable. I'm sorry."

It was quiet except for our boots. Even the red-winged blackbirds that would normally dart at anyone walking down these roads felt some sort of pity or fear of our strange amalgamation.

"When I lived in Paris, my roommate had a motorcycle like you. He was German. Every morning he had a shot of vodka. We had bunk beds and I'd watch him from the top bunk. I thought all white people started their day with a shot of vodka. Just like combing your hair or brushing your teeth." Medhi trailed off but started laughing, as if he'd silently continued the conversation.

"How did you end up in Wisconsin?" I asked.

"My wife. She started a medical practice here."

"She's a doctor?"

"Yes, as am I," Medhi said.

"And you don't want medical attention? I look behind me and I see blood trailing from your leg."

"Stop looking behind you," Medhi said.

* * *

Shortly after we got married, my wife and I visited friends who lived in a cabin on Mt. Baldy. It wasn't legal to rent anything on Mt. Baldy, but they'd made some sort of arrangement and got to live in this beautiful place with a stone chimney and waterfall outside their front deck. Driving up the switchbacks, you had to cross a fjord to get to their place. They'd moved there to teach and didn't have any friends. And living on a mountain was no way to make friends, but it was so beautiful. So they were trapped. They were so happy we visited, making all sorts of dinners with wine from nearby vineyards. They were making a statement about themselves, and it got a little overbearing and annoying, all this pent-up need to prove themselves. One day my wife and I decided we would wake up early and summit Mt. Baldy together. We didn't tell them our plans because there would be maps and advice and supplies. The climb wasn't all that treacherous, but we didn't bring enough water; we'd forgotten we were in a desert. An easy thing to do in Los Angeles. The last part of the hike you had to boulder up about 30 feet. She slipped and cut her hand in a jamb. I got to the summit first and helped her up. I kissed her hand as we looked out over the valley, and we shared a cigarette. We sat up there in the thin air for about fifteen minutes and she told me she thought everything was beautiful but scary. That the world could swallow her and no one would know. I told her I would never let that happen.

* * *

Medhi pointed ahead to a black Volvo station wagon. "There it is."

He had me help get his pants off. The cut wasn't too bad, but worse than he'd thought. It was dark red with dust and pebbles encrusted along the edges. He frowned, but began to clean it with water and tweezers. "Looks like I'll have to stitch this, but I can do that later," he said, and then he bandaged it. I asked him about the other leg. I told him I thought it was broken. He said it was a sprain, then grabbed some sort of ice pack that he smacked and taped around his thigh. Then he gingerly put some weight on it.

"You're not sleepy or anything are you?" he asked, and I told him I wasn't. "Good," he said, "then it's probably just a bump on your head you can brag to your wife about." We drove the road we'd just walked. Little drips of blood marked the way. As he drove I noticed something metal in his hand, like a coin.

"I still don't understand why a doctor wouldn't want to go to the hospital after ..."

"I also smoke, and I'm a doctor."

"Is that what you were reaching down to pick up when I hit you?" I asked and pointed at the coin he was twisting in his fingers.

He nodded.

"Is it a coin?"

"It's more than a coin." As Medhi said this he lit a smoke, and I noticed the song on the radio was the song he was chanting when I first found him.

"Hey. This is what you were chanting," I said, and he looked at me, smiled and exhaled. "It's what you said to me as I was coming to after the accident."

"Yes," Medhi said and turned it up a little. He sang along with it. "Do you want to know what I'm singing?" he asked and I said I did.

"You are so tired of this city without me."

I laughed and Medhi laughed.

"It's a Persian song my wife loves; she used to sing it to me. This coin that I was picking up is from her. It's my good luck charm. It helped me catch fish, but not any more," he said. Then he chucked it out the window, looked at me and smiled.

"It's important to know when something is no longer

good luck," he said.

* * *

"Do you think you can get that bike to run?" he asked as we pulled up to it.

I walked over to my bike. The fork looked like it was straight. The rim wasn't exactly true, but it seemed like it might be in good enough shape to get me into town. My phone rang again. It was my wife. I could tell by the ring. I answered. She called because she had a dream that I had crashed. It was a vivid morning dream.

I told her I was fine, just bumped my head a little bit. She told me she would pick me up. That I should stay put. I tried to tell her she didn't have to do that, but I knew I needed her. We hung up and I looked at Medhi. "She's coming to pick me up," I said to him. "Just have to figure what to do with the four hours it will take for her to get here."

"I suppose you could do some fishing," Medhi said. I nodded and smiled, then told him I would write out contact information for him so he could send me the bill for whatever treatment he needed. He said I'd done everything he asked and that he would take care of the rest. I thought about telling him he had no idea the extent of the damage, but stopped myself. He was a grown man and if he said he got what he wanted …We said an unceremonious goodbye.

I rolled my bike out of the reeds. I'd left the key in it. It started right up. I sat on it and listened to the engine's staccato rumble and thought about where I might fish. There was a river near the road. I turned the bike off. I had to hop a cattle fence, but there weren't any other impediments besides some tick-laden tall grass. The banks were mushy, which meant this area probably wasn't heavily fished. Maybe I was one of the first. There was a nice deep pool I was getting bites in. I spotted a sizeable rainbow hiding behind a rock where he could be lazy. I thought he'd seen me because he darted out, but the real reason made itself apparent. There was an otter making his way down the river, hanging and gnawing on the reeds. He drifted right past me, floating on his back. He would clear all the pools. I followed him as he paddled on his back along the edge. He seemed to be smiling at me with his black eyes. The river bent and I had to walk through it in some places where the banks were too overgrown. I had nowhere to be, so figured I'd follow this guy. He led me to the opening of a cave. I figured I'd be safe with waders and jeans on, so walked into the mouth of the cave. There was a slab of limestone inside that I sat on. It was nice and cool in there and I could hear water dripping from the porous walls. I thought back to something my wife and I tried to do a long time ago when we were separated. She had to drive to Ohio a lot to see her parents and the boredom could kill you on those trips, so we'd set up a time when we'd both think as hard as we could about the other and try to talk to each other, but not really talk, just think really deeply about the person. Later when we'd meet up we'd see if either of us could feel the other person at that time. So I decided that's what I would do in this cave. I would think intensely about my wife and try to talk to her. To see if I could somehow get into her head. I closed my eyes. At first everything was black and all I heard was water dripping, but then that Persian song about being tired of this city without you joined in, reverberating as if playing on a record player somewhere deep inside the cave. Then the otter entered, paddling along some dark water inside my head. I could see little blades of light in his onyx eyes, and he seemed to be laughing, not in the way otters always seem to be laughing, but in a more purposeful way. He was kicking along in rhythm to the Persian music. Once this all gathered I felt very relaxed until something inside me was warning me not to fall asleep. It was my wife's voice. It's dangerous to sleep after a concussion, she knew this. She knew all this stuff. But it felt so nice in that dark cave away from the local sunburned, sagging people who just stare at you as you pump gas from their stations.

Every good insurance man knows there are fewer acts of God in the Midwest. It made underwriting easier. The otter was whistling along to the Persian song in my head. Its paws were behind its head. It was wearing old Persian shoes, the kind with the tips pointed skyward. It was laughing and I was laughing. And the water and the ground shook to my wife's admonition. Don't fall asleep. I smiled at the otter, shook my head and opened my eyes. I had to wake up.

§

Skunk

MARIA LAY IN HER COTTON PAJAMAS, HER LIPS, SLIGHTLY ajar, have no color. She is dreaming a familiar dream: she is walking along a beachhead fifteen feet from the lip of Lake Erie and is about to pass a young girl bobbing on a spring hippo—the kind you find in a playground. The girl jerks the hippo forward, then falls back into its recoil in perfect rhythm with the Lake Erie waves patting the sand behind her, making it look as if the little girl is leading the waters in slow cavalry charge. Maria leans down to the little girl to ask her a question, a question she doesn't have the words for yet. As she bends down, she is hit by a rancid smell that has swarmed across the lake and now envelops her and the little girl. This wakes Maria. She opens her eyes to the dull morning light and that smell that was in her dream is now in her bedroom, blowing in through the window. She lay still for a few moments as the smell grows. She looks at her husband and finally decides to wake him when the smell is joined by loud caws from a pack of crows.

Bob, her husband, was dreaming about a thirty-foot long lobster attacking his and Maria's son. A pack of crows had just come to help him by distracting the giant lobster. When he wakes, he too is immediately hit by the smell. He sucks large chunks of air through his nostrils.

"What is that … that smell?"

"I don't know," Maria answers.

"Jesus,"says Bob.

* * *

Two crows fly past the window and land on the roof above the bedroom. Bob walks over to the window in his boxer shorts and t-shirt. Maria stares at the hairs on his legs, which point in all directions, and wonders why humans have the ugliest hair, like we're in some middle phase of evolution. She asks Bob what the crows are doing and gets no quick response; Bob stares out at them hectoring over something on the driveway. "I don't know," he finally says, while scratching the meaty piece of leg just below the tuck of his ass.

Five minutes later, Bob and Maria are both in robes and unfastened jogging shoes and are walking out to the driveway. The crows have circled around something at the apron near the newspaper. The smell has not abated and the sun seems too stubborn to yellow the morning light; it begins to feel as if this morning will not start until they find out why these fat black birds have converged on their driveway. They walk closer, making the crows scatter to the roof, and behind the curtain of black wing flaps lies the source of their olfactory assault: the cleanly decapitated head of a skunk facing them, as if it were buried up to its neck in driveway cement.

* * *

When Bob married Maria, his job had him traveling almost every week, inspecting the power plants that rope and smear the Great Lake shores of Ohio, Indiana and Michigan. Since Bob never really wanted to be married or familied, the intermittent wife and fathering by proxy seemed a smart compromise, and this is the way he grew his life.

Bob liked the road life and his tan government-issued Ford. He liked joking with the front desk employees at hotels, liked eating alone at chain restaurants. These things were so drab and so meek, they almost begged him to destroy them, to piss on the floor, to beat on them; they weren't precious like a family. He liked the cloying smiles beamed from the foremen at the plants, his perfect children, who would have to rearrange the heating of their microwave lunches according to him. He liked having his house, his wife, his garage and his mailbox all in a flat suburb, all removed.

His life moved quickly for a while and he was pleased. But after seven years, the hotels and their windowless bathrooms grew weary. The Ford shed its government-issued smell. He needed to make a change, so he planted himself in an office downtown where he would talk on the phone, process papers and drink water. And as Bob drank his water, the decreasing biological distinction between him and the spider plant in his office was not lost upon him. He neglected mentioning to his intermittent wife, Maria, that he no longer needed to travel for work. Instead, he rented an apartment in the industrial part of town, one that overlooked an abandoned steel mill, and lived there three days a week. From the window of Bob's new apartment he could see the waffled metal that made up the façade of the mill. He could peer into one of the windows at a string of lights. He imagined working in that mill, sunk below Cleveland, in the wet and dark. He imagined carts with cast iron wheels whipping around, and large men in tall rooms dissecting stones with torches and clamps under revolving metal buckets brimmed with heavy amber fluid. It all seemed so unlike the frozen smiles and cubed fluorescent lighting of his office. He imagined sitting in the back of some workmate's truck getting high and laughing with squinty eyes over the prospect of making double pay on the fourth of July. He imagined having sex with the breasts of derelict woman who smelled like gin and laughed at his jokes in this apartment that overlooked that steel mill. But he only imagined this. He never summoned his genitalia for any communal work; it was used mostly to direct his urine into that strange blue water sitting listlessly in his commode.

* * *

The skunk's eyes were still glassy, Maria pointed out, surveying the yard for a stick she could use as a pointer. There was no gore around the head. "This must have just happened," Maria said as Bob stared.

The newspaper, rolled in its blue cellophane, sat near the head of the skunk, making it look like some perverse Wiffle ball set left on the apron of their driveway. Bob sucked in air through his nose and tried to think of a more sanctimonious way of clearing the head from the driveway than lifting it with a shovel into a black trash bag. While Bob pondered, Maria found a twig in the yard and walked it back toward the skunk head.

"Where do you think the rest of him is?"

"Do you think the crows carried it to the roof—the body?" asked Maria. Bob just stared as Maria used the small branch to slowly close the skunk's glassy eyes.

"I suppose I can check the roof," Bob said. And it was quiet for a bit. Both Bob and Maria let their minds wander as the sun let out some of its color. They stood looking out over their yard and the road in front until the sound of a garage door intruded and goaded them back to their morning routines.

* * *

Maria's Body

Throughout high school, Maria was asked on one date. She remembers her father opening the door to reveal her shiny date holding a corsage. She remembers her father pointing at the corsage in its plastic box and asking her date if he could eat that. Maria's clothes, her hair, her walk—all emblems of the awkward internal battle she waged daily with her body and its lengthening and swelling that didn't seem to jibe with what should have been genetically prescribed. She looked nothing like her five-foot-one mother, nothing like her two pimply, sporting brothers, nothing like her dentist father. The boys at school were intimidated by her obnoxious breasts, which her ridiculously baggy sweaters were unable to quiet, and the girls simply hated her for those breasts. Maria was alone with her body to course through school with the tension of an angry couple trying to look civil at a dinner party—until she moved away.

Maybe it was exasperation; maybe her body had worn her out by the time she was 19 and away. This is one explanation for how Maria's body came to no longer crowd her. It had won the argument, leaving her to simply assuage as it moved on and ripped through the drunken, fawning boys. Maria grew to enjoy steering this power through the loins of all the stumbling boys—she never went for the aggressive types—but after time it grew a bit disconcerting that she actually had this power, that it was so unsupervised and arbitrary; was she supposed to believe that she deserved this? She started feeling something, started dreaming something. She dreamt that she was plunged by some burp in the force of gravity to the bottom of a green lake. Maria couldn't figure out what this dream meant, but she felt sure these nocturnal images her mind kept dropping came from some thoughtful source telling her she needed to change, or to adapt—an overdue notice, but something biological, not spiritual. Maria ate different foods, exercised more, paid someone to tattoo a frog on her shoulder blade. She read self-improvement books by toothy balding authors, but the green great lake still lay waiting to swallow her come night. She decided that perhaps some spiritual rendering was needed. An ablution. She felt an urge to kneel before the meshed face of a priest, to bow her head below his pendulous adam's apple and receive the garlicky wind of his penance. She wanted to unmuddle her life before her life's divine audience, to curry the favor of that audience, which she felt could be responsible for her nightly plunging.

She went to a church away from campus to get away from "campus ministry" forever stung with the onus of trying to be contemporary. She had to take a bus to the church and sit with the crumpled service industry workers with their grocery bagged lunches. These same bags you could see everywhere in the city: tumbling across streets, slung over antennae. Maria could stare without thinking at all the subdued faces obliquely reflected in the scratched plastine windows of the bus, as they were shuttled to or from a hopeless and bald section of town where the billboards are lower and pitch mentholated cigarettes. In the winter she would pray for the seat in the back above the heater where, for the thirty-minute ride, she could be consumed by the chewbaccal growl of the engine and the heat it dispensed between her legs. The church provided no comfort that could match this. The constant addition and subtraction of bodies to the roving corridor helped Maria realize that there were more people in the world than those swimming predictably in her small and stupid circle. The dream soon stopped. Actually, it placed her on the shore of a quiet Lake Erie beach, out of harm. The dream moved forward.

* * *

Bob scissored his leg out the bedroom window and onto the roof. The crows flew away again, this time to a tree. He walked to where they were gathered and found nothing. He looked out over the street, cocking his leg and placing his hand over his hip so that it would have looked to anyone below as if his house were a bear he'd just slain and was now standing proudly upon.

* * *

Bob's Other Apartment

It was May in Cleveland, and a day that began placidly progressed into a warm evening with the chance of a thunderstorm at bedtime. The warmth was welcome after a long winter; it inspired strangers to talk on elevators. And Bob was spending it on his bed watching a flaccid baseball game on television before deciding to walk over to the gas station near his apartment for some food and to perhaps thumb the magazines. He walked to the gas station where he saw a woman in cotton sweatpants holding a jug of milk in front of her car. Down the road sat the steel mill; he would walk toward that.

The street became more gravelly with tufts of grass poking out like unbarbered pubic hair as the road descended toward the mill. Bob walked off the road and into a meadow where fat power lines hung high in the air under a yellowing sky. A tall fence crowned with barbed wire enclosed the mill and its parking lot. Bob wrung his fingers through the holes of the fence and peered through at the one small car that held a walrus of a man unscrewing a thermos and listening to the baseball game. Looking down the fence, Bob saw a section that was cut away and peeled back. He crouched through the opening, then sat for a while on a small hill cloaked by a tree branch. Bob wanted in that mill. And he knew the world was shrinking of places in which he wanted in. His son would be nine in less than a week and here he was crouched on some hill on a forgotten patch of earth. Another vehicle pulled into the lot. Bob watched as the two men got out of their idling cars and talked. One of the men saw him on the hill and pointed to the other; then they were both staring at him from about 200 yards away. Bob decided it was time to split, so he got up and slowly walked back through the hole in the fence.

* * *

Maria stood looking out the window above the kitchen sink for any sign of the skunk's remains. More and more cars passed on the street as the morning progressed. Maria thought that maybe a truck had run the skunk over and popped the head out onto the driveway. But there'd have to be some gory stamp left behind. Wouldn't there?

Maria recalled the story her father told her about a chicken that lived for fours years without its head. The chicken became a celebrity with photo spreads in both *Time* and *Life*; it toured the country in different freak shows and inspired other farmers tired of being farmers to whack diagonal cuts into the necks of their livestock.

The owners kept their prize bird alive with an eyedropper to dispense food and clear its larynx. But the headless chicken that lived like a celebrity also died like one, choking on its own corn-kernel vomit in a motel room. Maria loved this story because it came from her dad, who usually would feel it out of decorum to tell such a grisly story with an ambiguous moral, but told it anyway.

* * *

Back in his apartment, Bob made his bed. He straightened his chest of drawers, the only piece of furniture aside from a chair and a bed frame. He counted and sorted the coins on top of his chest of drawers. He wanted in that building. Bob looked at his alarm clock. 8:17. He added the numbers to 25, subtracted them to 9. He shut his eyes so the digital red would blur. He really wanted in that building. He changed into a black sweater then looked at his reflection in the mirror. His hair was a bird's nest. He messed it up more, then walked out of his apartment as the yellow spring light started darkening, signaling that maybe the rain wouldn't come.

There was a scrap yard in back of the steel mill where Bob figured he could sneak through. Bob hopped the fence in a section without barbed wire, then walked past a large mound of refrigerators and car bumpers all rusting into one another like a stalagmite. Up ahead stood a big garage door and a strange white truck with wheels in front, treads in the back, and a large grabbing device for a nose. It looked like a giant pair of pliers. Bob hopped into the driver's chair and looked out at the different mounds of scraps sitting like dust piles. Dusk receded into night, and Bob could see the sodium lamps, now lit, reflecting in the globs of metal. He imagined what it would feel like to clear the yard of all this scrap. Behind him was a window that looked into the shop. He looked in through it then pushed it open.

Inside the shop, a dim floodlight washed over the room. Lathes stood against the right wall and larger machines lined the left, making a walkway down the middle. The ceiling stood thirty feet high; the windows were above eye level along the top. The place had a caged-in sort of smell, but it didn't seem to have the decrepit grandeur that Bob thought it should have. It was just a room with a couple different machines in it. No ghosts. He didn't even feel like he was in a place he wasn't supposed to be in, but he was. There was a chair near one of the lathes, Bob sat in it and let the room get quiet, maybe then the place could somehow reveal itself, he thought. In front of the plant, pitched into the ground like a flagpole, stood a steel truck gear, about fifteen feet tall. The mill made this gear, and the obsolescence of that gear brought about the obsolescence of the mill. Bob let his mind go blank. He heard a door open and the light click on. Bob turned in the chair to see the two men he'd seen in the parking lot pointing flashlights at him. He stood up quickly. They looked at one another for a second before Bob took off running for the window that he'd climbed in through. They two men watched as Bob swerved through the piles of metal in the yard. Watched Bob's body, bent like parentheses, scale the tall fence then arch gingerly over the barbed wire. Minutes later, Bob was back at his apartment. Maria was waiting for him outside his door.

She wanted to know if he was cheating on her. She knew he wasn't, but asked anyway. She wanted to know if anyone else knew about this place? He answered truthfully. No one knew and there was no one else. She stared at him for a while then looked away, deciding simply to accept her lot and move on. They would never talk about it, or the underpinning awkwardness that they shared. Maria was happy with her life. It wasn't perfect but it felt right. She didn't want to change anything.

* * *

Maria's parents lobbied ferociously for their grandchild to be sent through Catholic schooling. They would pay the tuition; help with car pool, etc. Bob wasn't happy about this, he felt it was an annoying intrusion, but he conceded because it meant a lot to Maria.

The first year went without incident, aside from the day their son came home and announced to his Maria that he had the devil in him. Maria told him not to joke about things like that, but neglected to ask him where he'd heard that. During the second year of schooling, the son started getting into trouble. He was talking when he wasn't supposed to, he threw a shoe at the blackboard, and, this morning while waiting in line during bathroom break, he brandished his privates at the boy standing behind him in line. Minutes later, the assistant principal was dialing the number of Maria's office.

Upon entering the principal's office, Maria apologized profusely. She did everything she could to feign the elongated look of shock she had practiced in the rearview mirror of her car. The principal offered a dour look in return. To the principal of St. Stanislaus Elementary, modern parents who procreated late in life were like tourists constantly visiting their children, constantly amazed by the unamazing. And regarding the administration of discipline: they were as limp as defrosted chicken breasts, wholly unable to brand their kids with the type of character that inspired healthy civilization.

It was reprehensible, he felt. And there was very little he, the principal, could do; the law tied his hands from any impactful disciplinary measures. But other hands were available. He invited Maria to sit down across from him, then slowly admonished her on the gravity of her son's forbidden exposition of privates in the hallway. Maria shook her head quickly, said the I knows and the I'm so sorrys to quicken this conversation the principal seemed to relish in torturing her with. He asked Maria if she really cared about correcting her son's behavior, asked her if she was committed to the proper growth of her son. Maria nodded, knowing very well the principal was constructing some sort of trap. The principal paused, shifted his legs, then told Maria that her son's "vivacity would, one day, work to his benefit … once properly steered." Maria moved her head up and down, happy to wrest away any sort of pride she could in her boy.

The principal then glided the deep, side drawer of his desk open, paused, and glanced into the drawer. "Why don't we go see your son?" the principal said, then lifted from the depths of that drawer a wooden paddle that was full of holes, making it look like a long slice of petrified swiss cheese. He handed the confusing piece of wood to Maria, then quietly led her to a room in the back where her boy was. Before reaching that room the principal paused, bathing her in his aftershave. "Be sure to explain to him why you are doing this, and be firm."

Maria nodded to the last morsel of instruction. The principal put his hand on her shoulder and Maria felt an intense and strange wave of arousal, something she did not want and would later feel miserable because of. She felt this strange combination of emotions once before when she was fifteen. She was sitting inside the smallish car of her track coach one afternoon after practice where she waited, out of the rain, for her late parents to pick her up. The seconds were wavering to the loud heat spilling out of the vents and over her pink legs, lightly coated in autumn rain. When her parents finally pulled their car into the lot, the part of Maria that reacted was the one that quickly opened the smallish car's door without saying a goodbye or thank you and ran to her parents' car, completely terrified.

The principal opened the door for Maria, who looked in at her son's legs dangling off a padded olive green bench. She walked in with the paddle at hip length on her right side, then sat next to her son and asked him what happened. Her boy smiled with a reddened face and cycled his legs as if he were wading. Maria sat looking at her child with his hands on the edge of the couch. Maybe it was the green bench along with the wading that reminded Maria of the dream, the plunging. With her index finger, she lifted her boy's chin and told him he should not show what's inside his pants to any of the kids in school. Then she stood up, lifted the paddle and swacked the end of the bench three times.

* * *

While walking in from the roof, Bob thought he saw something black with a splotch of white twisted in the neighbor's shrub. He turned around and walked toward the edge so that his eyes could sharpen on whatever it was on top of the bush. He walked closer, and in his excitement, slipped on a roof tile. He was able to catch the gutter as he fell and dragged it down with him. Maria, staring out the kitchen window thinking about a headless chicken, heard the aluminum detach and the thud of her husband. She ran out of the house to find Bob lying in the grass below a hanging white gutter that looked like a long bony finger pointing directly at her husband. Half of Bob's face was wrinkled in pain as he calmly told his wife that at least one of his legs was broken. Maria ran back inside for the phone. Lying there alone, Bob arched his neck back so he could get a clear look at his neighbor's bush. From inside Maria heard what she thought was rolling vocalized pain, a type she'd never heard from her husband, but it was actually something closer to laughter. She ran out with the phone to see her husband pointing at the neighbor's shrub. "There it is," he said pointing at the body of the skunk.

§

The Pot Roast Consultant

THIN BLOODLESS STRIPS OF BEEF SIZZLED IN THE MIDDLE of the table over a small grated gas fire that Keiko tended with chopsticks. She turned the stiffening patches of meat, then plucked them from the fire to the plates of Andrew and her husband Yuichi, who let the meat stack as he chain-smoked Hope cigarettes over a mirrored ashtray and conversed clumsily with Andrew about hanger steak and cormorant fishing. Andrew conversed as best he could, trying not to stare at Keiko and the yellows and oranges the fire painted across her poreless face as she slid the lever in front that made the fire rise then sink between Andrew and her husband.

The waitress returned with a plate of raw caribou and octopus meat, framed perfectly between a tight smile and nude pantyhose. Keiko accepted the plate then smiled in Andrew's direction as Yuichi lit another Hope. Andrew could have watched Keiko burn things all night, but he had a conversation to seem excited about.

Andrew is a pot roast consultant, employed by Rolling Pasture Ranch, Glenview, Illinois. He was sent to Nagoya to explore a tax dodge a rising star at the office conceived. Distributors pay an enormous tax to import beef to Japan; a tax that individuals aren't assessed. So Andrew was sent to create a "pot roast club" and pool individuals who would receive a group shipment. It probably wouldn't work, but it was something to try, seemed to be the sentiment at the office, and that was expressed through headlong confidence in it. Keiko and Yuichi were leads he was given. Andrew's boss tried to inspire him to think bigger, beyond the tax dodge. "Imagine a picture: An advertisement from the fifties, one with an aproned wife bending into a hot oven, behind her stands her angled and dapper husband. Now what we're going to do is take this picture and insert Japanese faces." Andrew thought of the picture and he tried to put Yuichi and Keiko in it, but it wasn't working all that well.

Andrew wanted to go to Japan badly and was good at sales. He liked talking and guessing at how people would react to different things. What they'd laugh at. What they'd buy. But in Nagoya he simply felt lost. Not unhappy or incurious, just unable to lash productivity to curiosity. He would not be able to engage his leads with good salesmanship, he knew, but he drifted through the motions.

The rainy season officially ended two nights ago and everyone seemed happy to see the sun, which now beamed a very wet heat over the stacked concrete of Nagoya. Andrew talked generically about this with Yuichi, who looked maybe 40 years old, but was north of 60; his wife Keiko was 38. Andrew lived in the same building as them, on the sixth floor of a concrete high rise, 25 miles from downtown Nagoya. The building squatted on pink concrete legs over a parking garage with a spot for every tenant who knew it was OK to live in a piece of shit apartment as long as you had a nice car. Every unit came with a balcony caged in chicken wire to deter the large crows that had been feasting on the powdery necks of old ladies all over Nagoya. It made the news nightly—septuagenarians nearly plucked off the ground by enormous crows, like reverse storks. Andrew thought about the crows and about how he had enough Cryovac bags of black angus to fill a waterbed as he sat on his balcony watching the television towers and alleys blink their red lights in some strange language across Nagoya.

Yuichi had a Toyota Crown Deluxe—brand new, he explained, lingering a bit to impress the detail upon Andrew who poured showa over the twitching strips Keiko set before him. "30,000 American dollars," Yuichi said without flinching, then dropped a cigarette into the thin layer of water at the bottom of the ashtray.

The last cry of Yuichi's cigarette and Andrew's "hmmph" synchronized. Andrew offered to pay for the meal, but was denied the proper three times. Keiko took care of the bill with the yen-stuffed envelope Yuichi handed her. It was an old tradition; a man never involved himself in monetary transactions. Keiko excused herself to the toilet as Yuichi and Andrew walked to the door through the staff's chorus of cloying appreciation. They walked to the back of the parking lot and stood in front of a small bamboo forest, breathing in the dense smoke of burning flesh blowing out the back of the restaurant.

Yuichi's telephone rang. "Mooshimoosh," he answered, then giggled over patchy conversation. Without warning, he handed Andrew the phone. Andrew's Japanese never worked over the phone. He needed eyes, gestures, physical context and a decent connection. He heard a young girl's voice on the other end. The phone crackled, then swirled. Yuichi laughed at his befuddlement, taking his phone back then barking a "baibai" as Keiko walked out the door. She smiled when she saw them in front of the dense forest of green bamboo tubes. It was a wonderful smile, Andrew thought—most of her teeth pointing everywhere but up and down, her eyes pierced.

The pink-legged high rise was just down the street. During the walk home, Yuichi explained to Keiko that he was going to bring Andrew somewhere else as Andrew stared into the window of the veterinary hospital next door. Every day he walked by that hospital teeming with shaved and mangled pets wrapped in casts or collared with cones on display in the window for some reason. A statement on how silly and adorable it was to be weak and cute.

Yuichi looked back at Andrew then slapped his shoulder. "Whiskey?"

"Hai," he said, then bowed to Keiko and wished her a good night.

They got into Yuichi's $30,000 Crown Deluxe and drove through the legs of the parking lot. Andrew caught himself doing things like this a lot in Nagoya, drifting into extended social engagements that he should have politely cut off. So people felt the need to continue entertaining him, bringing him deeper into the stranger corners of the gridded city.

The streets and alleys were dotted with red lights sewn into the pavement and blinking in the darkness. Yuichi drove quickly, happy to display the agility of his Crown Deluxe. Andrew asked him who the girl on the phone was.

"Ahh Maki-tyan," Yuichi said smiling.

"Your daughter?" Andrew asked which made Yuichi laugh and say nothing.

They stopped in front of a place that had a red paper lantern lit in front. Yuichi quickly slid the door open and crossed into the barrage of welcomes like oral sabers crossed above, funneling him and Yuichi in. Yuichi led Andrew to a table in back of the bar, past a plump Japanese girl singing "Like a Rolling Stone" karaoke. Her eyes were fixed on the prompter screen displaying a video of a waterfall montage around Bob Dylan's katakana'd lyrics. Everyone drank their beers and ate small fish pizzas without mind to the chubby girl who looked up from the screen to shout the refrain.

Yuichi had a waitress in kimono bring a bottle of Jack Daniels. "From Tennessee," she said. Yuichi flipped through his wallet as the waitress carefully poured the two whiskeys, then placed the bottle on the table. Yuichi pulled out a small picture of a young Japanese girl sitting rigidly on a striped couch. The girl was smiling perfectly, her teeth all straight and white. Yuichi, smiling also, asked what he thought of her. Andrew said she was pretty. Unsatisfied, Yuichi asked if she was his type, to which Andrew shrugged and said sure.

"You probably don't like Japanese women, huh?" he said.

"No. No. I do."

"You like hourglass," Yuichi said, then moved his hands in the silhouette of a curvy woman. "And you have a girlfriend in Chicago, right?"

"Yes," Andrew said smiling.

"But she is in Chicago."

The whiskey tasted too sweet for Andrew, and Yuichi spent more time praising the quality of the American whiskey than drinking it. Yuichi explained he had to drink slowly or he'd get the red face, then dropped another Hope into the ashtray. His cell phone rang again. He answered, then laughed and looked toward a lady walking in. She was the same lady as in the picture. "Ahh Maki-tyan." Yuichi spoke with a breathy voice into the phone at Maki, who sauntered in smiling with her pink cell phone elegantly lit on the side of her face.

She looked more perfect in person. She was thin and angled dramatically; her hair hung low in black waves, so black you could see purple strewn in. They bowed to one another and she put out her hand for him to shake, then displayed that perfect smile as she sat down gingerly with her back straight as if she were about to play the piano. She moved very little as she spoke, and used her round brown eyes the way Yukiko had used the fire—they'd rise, then sink. Yuichi took pride in Maki's presence with more smiles, more laughs. He massaged her shoulders as she made small talk with Andrew. The waitress brought her a pink martini and Yuichi some green tea. Maki took perfectly executed small sips with two hands— one below the base, and one along the curved cup.

After the first drink, Andrew felt everyone staring at him, as if they were all waiting for something they knew would happen. They weren't just hanging out. Their eyes moved to Maki, who looked directly at Andrew.

"We would like to talk to you about a job." Maki said, then handed Andrew a piece of paper. Andrew scanned it:

We want you to cooperate with us in finding girl who would like to be filmed doing natural things, like dressing for bedtime.

* * *

Andrew's Current Job description: Bo-eki *International Trade*

Andrew had failed miserably on his last mission. He drove through the Aichi prefecture to meet with a group of house-wives who were interested in receiving pot roast consultation from a young American. They seemed pleased to see his tall thick body constructed from years of pot roast consumption. He came armed with cooking instructions written in Japanese, cartoon pictures of cows with big dopey smiles, butchers' diagrams, and slanted nutritional information. He had little diplomas with black heifer silhouette designs for the wives who could successfully cook a virtual roast and pair it with appropriate vegetables. The diplomas sat next to a cooler that held 15 bags of rump. Andrew stood with a tan microphone in front of the rapt ladies. Any of these women could have been a model for his company's dream picture. He held up one of the bagged roasts. He showed it to the crowd for their approval, and they were all interested. They gathered around the meat. One lady had a question.

"What is the purple liquid in the bag?" It took him a little while, but with the help of one of the ladies upfront pointing directly at the blood he understood.

"That's blood. Cow blood."

"Why purple?" she asked.

"It's purple because there is no oxygen in the bag. If you look at the blood in your veins it, too, looks purple because there is no oxygen around it. See?" he held up his arm. But as he looked out over the sea of wives he could sense the confusion. He got out one of his steak knives, cut into the bag and let the red blood run over his hand, then held it up for everyone to see. Across the crowd hands covered mouths. Some muted shrieks bounced around as droplets of blood dotted the stage.

Back in Yuichi's $30,000 Crown Deluxe

Andrew thanked Yuichi for the offer and promised to think about it. Maki opened the door of the Crown for Andrew, and they headed home. The car ride was quiet until Yuichi reached into the middle console of the Crown for a blue toothbrush that had only one row of bristles. He ran the brush loudly over his teeth.

Andrew daydreamed over the swoosh of the brush, and somehow unwillingly his head rolled back to Chicago, back to the parking lot of Rolling Pasture Ranch. He remembered talking with Al, the overnight security guard who watched grainy footage of dry aging bovine carcasses that would be sent to Japan, where they could demand a ridiculous sum. When Al heard the company was sending Andrew to Japan, he said he needed to show him something. Al showed up every night a half hour early for his shift. He hadn't called in sick in over three years. He wobbled in, tidily dressed in his polyester Rolling Pasture uniform that couldn't contain the dank armpit stench that collided with the smell of a bologna and cheese sandwich his wife prepared for him every night, and a thermos of discount scotch he prepared for himself every night. Al was a dependable employee who got drunk every night watching black and white security camera footage of dangling cold beef carcasses.

"I got something to show you," he told Andrew. "I'll bring it in tomorrow," he said. The next night after Al set his bologna sandwich and thermos on the control panel he walked Andrew outside with an excitement that showed he'd probably waited all day for this. They walked to his old tan Impala that encapsulated in more dense form the smell of cheap scotch, bologna and rotting flesh. Al popped the trunk and above the spare, lit by a dimming trunk light, lay what looked like a samurai sword.

"Wow," Andrew said, then reached for the sword. Al moved closer to Andrew, looked up and smiled into him with his small yellow teeth. "Go on, touch it," Al said.

"Where'd you get this Al?" Andrew asked grabbing the handle, wanting to end this.

"It's from the war," he said slowly, then coughed for five seconds. "Pull it out," he said, and Andrew did as was told. The blade was old and dull, but still reflected the light from the parking lot lamps and Impala.

"Do you see it?" Al asked, his voice reverberating in the trunk.

"Yeah, I see it," Andrew replied as Al crouched closer and ran his finger, which now held a Lucky Strike, over the edge of the exposed blade to the top where he stopped at a brown blemish.

"You know what that is? That's Jap blood," he said, bending in the trunk too close to Andrew, bathing him in cheap scotch vapor. "I got 'em with his own sword," he said, and lifted his lip over his ancient teeth. Al's smile was pulled out of the frame in Andrew's conscious by the sound of moaning within the ergonomically designed cabin of the Crown Deluxe.

He looked at Maki in the backseat—her arms folded neatly over her legs. Smiling her smile. He looked at Yuichi, who was still pulverizing his enamels with the toothbrush. The moan seemed to be coming from the space between the toothbrush now arched upwards and the open mouth of Yuichi. It took a while, but he finally got it. "Moonriver." Yuichi was moaning Moonriver.

At a stoplight, Yuichi turned to Andrew, wet toothbrush in hand. "You want to just work in beef, right?"

"Umm," Andrew said.

"Is it interesting?"

"Sometimes," he said.

"How much do you get paid?" Yuichi asked abruptly.

"I do all right," Andrew said."

Yuichi grunted, then put the Crown Deluxe in park.

"Gochisosemadesita," said Andrew, thanking him for the food and whiskey, then shut the car door.

Andrew changed clothes and lay on the tatami mat before the TV in his apartment. From the corner of his eye, he could see the fax machine, the nexus between him and his mustachioed boss sitting in Chicago behind his fake maple desk topped with a brass bull paperweight. The tray was empty, but Andrew knew it would soon fill with new instructions, new nudges and passive aggressions, and if matters stayed on pace it wouldn't be long before that mustachioed boss called him back to Chicago to troll through Red Lobster and Ponderosa parking lots negotiating shit beef with franchise managers. He turned the television on.

The Nagoya Dragons were battling the Tokyo Giants in Japanese baseball. It was 3-3 in the bottom of the ninth with the Dragons at bat, one out and the bases loaded. The Dragons were a working class baseball team, and Andrew grew to like them. They were the Japanese White Sox, he figured. The Tokyo Giants were a big money team with endless resources and a brooding Darth Vader-like manager. They were the Japanese Yankees, Andrew convinced himself, and easily vilified them. A white guy was batting for the Dragons. Every team in the league was allowed to import two Americans. The strike zone is much smaller than the American one; it's a hitter's game. The white guy had driven the count to two balls and no strikes, a pitch to hit. He would get a fastball to smash, and he did. He smashed it right to the shortstop, who caught it, then stepped on second to complete the double play.

"Shit!" Andrew yelled, then got up for the last Kirin in the miniature fridge. He never left a tied game. Once he sat in the stands of old Commiskey Park for six and a half hours. White Sox versus Indians—both teams were out of contention, but it didn't matter. Andrew sat down on the tatami, ready for the tenth when a Samurai movie came on. He thought it might be an advertisement, but it wasn't. The game was over. No extra innings. Andrew felt a surge of hatred similar to what he felt at the end of a trip to Montreal when he spent his last ten bucks on pate thinking it would be something like a patty melt. Shortly after came a knock at the door revealing a perfectly coifed young lady erect on black high heels. Maki.

"Sitzudesimasu," she said, apologizing for appearing at the door. She removed her heels and walked into the apartment, which displayed a collage of dry cleaning bags, dirty laundry, and various beef paraphernalia.

"You are alone, right?" she asked in English, while peering around all three rooms of the apartment, stopping at the grand piano in the main room. "Oh, you play piano?" she asked, smiling with her perfect teeth.

"I can't play. It came with the apartment," Andrew said.

"My grandfather bought me a grand piano like this when I was three years old. I can't play well," Maki said, covering her mouth with her hand. "My Grandfather bought me the piano because he wanted me to be an elegant lady, Andrew-san," Maki said, then pulled the cover to expose the shiny keys. "What do you think, Andrew-san, am I an elegant lady?"

He told her she was an elegant lady.

"So what does Andrew-san think about Yuich-san?"

"Seems like a very ... interesting person."

"Yes, I think so, too. And what does Andrew-san think about working for Yuich-san?"

"I haven't really thought about it."

"He's very rich. I know you have a job, but you can work at night for Yuich-san," Maki said, then slid her pantyhosed legs in front of the brass piano pedals. "Two days ago, Yuich-san called me. He said you moved in. He spoke fondly of his new American neighbor." Maki paused here, and Andrew's eyes were drawn to her legs. Maki took notice of Andrew's eyes. "He believes there is a definite reason for this, a reason that you moved next door. He believes you are part of his future. He told me this again tonight after speaking with you. He wants your help, and certainly somehow he can help you. He is a rich and wise man."

"What exactly does Yuichi-san do for a living?"

"Men's clothing. He was one of the first in Nagoya with neckties. He owned 140 stores on Honshu not long ago. Now he owns 75, but he has a new idea, and he would like you to help him. He wants to start a business on the Internet, and he wants to find women willing to be filmed to attract more viewers to his site. Men like to watch women change and masturbate."

"Ahh. That's probably true, and I'm very flattered, Maki, but I don't know if I'm the right person."

"That doesn't matter."

"No?"

"He believes there is a reason. You should think about his offer. He'll pay you a lot of money. He may seem a little crazy, but he is as you say: a very interesting person. You are someone girls would say yes to. You will say you're from Los

Angeles, and they will all want to be filmed."

"What?"

"I don't want to talk more about this, Andrew-san. Here is a letter I've translated for you from Yuich-san."

Andrew took the letter from Maki and began to open it when Maki delicately grabbed his wrist and said, "Maybe I could play a song on the piano. Would you like to hear the song before you open that envelope?"

Andrew said yes.

"Tonight, be the first taifu for you?" Maki asked, then began to play an up-tempo song that made Andrew feel like he was on a game show.

"Taifu, what's taifu?" Andrew asked, to which Maki was silent. Instead of asking again, he walked to get his dictionary out of the kitchen. "Taifu," he said over and over again. "Typhoon," the dictionary explained. Andrew closed the book. He walked back to Maki who was playing a Beethoven sonata.

"Typhoon tonight?" he asked. Maki just smiled at him as she played. "How will you get home?"

Maki tilted her head and smiled at Yuichi.

Andrew looked through his apartment for sheets and a pillow to the sounds of Maki's piano, then turned off the light and sat down to drink his beer. He turned the Samurai movie back on only to find it was interrupted by a newscast announcing the imminent taifu that was hitting just north of Tokyo. He looked outside — the red lights from the television tower still blinked. He laid on the futon, holding his beer more than drinking it, and fell asleep as Maki played a Chopin nocturne.

Hours later he woke to the sound of wind ripping through the corridor. Maki was awake and bent over Andrew's semi-erect penis that somehow snaked its way out of the opening of Andrew's boxer shorts. She seemed to be measuring it against her hand. Andrew sat up, startling Maki, who smiled nervously and then laid back down, her head now inches from Andrew's.

"It just came out while you were sleeping," Maki said covering her smile with her thin hand. "You had very nice dreams, Andrew-san," Maki continued, as Andrew snafued his penis back through the boxer hole and stood up. He walked to the fridge for his water jug and wolfed down a pint in a few swallows. It was the best thing he'd ever tasted. Andrew could see the yellow envelope Maki handed him last night on the kitchen table. He also saw a new fax sitting in the tray. The wind was absurdly loud as it cut through the corridor. Andrew looked for his sweatpants, then noticed Maki had them on so he walked outside the door in his boxers. It was 5:47 in the morning when he opened the pink apartment door and walked into the wind tunnel. He searched for the mouth of the wind tunnel, where there was an opening for the stairs. He sat in front of them. The sky was yellow and pink, and the bamboo forest across the street thrashed furiously. Papers blew in fast circles on the street and rain seemed to be falling sideways. No one was outside. Over the wind Andrew could hear chanting from inside the apartment near the stairs, and he could smell with an acute morning nose incense seeping out the bottom of the door. It smelled like pepper and burning wood—it was the same incense used at the Buddhist temples he'd visited in Kyoto. Andrew listened to the wind rip through the streets and corridor. While his boxer shorts rippled, he looked through the stairwell at the yellows and pinks of the tumultuous Nagoya sky. If he sold no beef, he at least had this.

He walked back to his apartment. Maki was asleep or pretending to be. He laid next to her, making sure his freshly measured penis was secure, then fell back asleep.

§

Ryan Kenealy currently lives in Evanston with his wife and two sons. He began his career selling novelty items at a flea market on a dirty street near Cleveland Hopkins Airport and has since worked for the circus in Chicago and sold pot roast in Japan. These stories originally appeared in *Open City*, *Another Chicago Magazine* and *Bridge*, among others. This is his first collection of stories.